A Note from the Author

Only You was included in the *Ever My Love* anthology in which six *USA Today* bestselling authors traced the history of the Lucius Ring from Roman times to the present. My story (*Only You*) features the ring in the late 1700s. *Ever My Love* was available to the public for only one month.

Now each author's story is available individually, along with the original prologue by the fabulous Kathryn Le Veque. Many thanks to Kathryn for allowing me to use her story in which the legend of the ring begins.

Some of the praise for Cheryl Bolen's writing:

"One of the best authors in the Regency romance field today." – *Huntress Reviews*

"Bolen's writing has a certain elegance that lends itself to the era and creates the perfect atmosphere for her enchanting romances." – *RT Book Reviews*

The Counterfeit Countess (Brazen Brides, Book 1)
Daphne du Maurier award finalist for Best Historical Mystery

"This story is full of romance and suspense. . . No one can resist a novel written by Cheryl Bolen. Her writing talents charm all readers. Highly recommended reading! 5 stars!" – *Huntress Reviews*

"Bolen pens a sparkling tale, and readers will adore her feisty heroine, the arrogant, honorable Warwick and a wonderful cast of supporting characters." – *RT Book Reviews*

One Golden Ring (Brazen Brides, Book 2)
"*One Golden Ring*...has got to be the most PERFECT Regency Romance I've read this year." – *Huntress Reviews*

Holt Medallion winner for Best Historical, 2006

Lady By Chance (House of Haverstock, Book 1)
Cheryl Bolen has done it again with another sparkling Regency romance. . .Highly recommended – *Happily Ever After*

The Bride Wore Blue (Brides of Bath, Book 1)
Cheryl Bolen returns to the Regency England she knows so well. . .If you love a steamy Regency with a fast pace, be sure to pick up *The Bride Wore Blue*. – *Happily Ever After*

With His Ring (Brides of Bath, Book 2)
"Cheryl Bolen does it again! There is laughter, and the interaction of the characters pulls you right into the book. I look forward to the next in this series." – *RT Book Reviews*

The Bride's Secret (Brides of Bath, Book 3)
(originally titled *A Fallen Woman*)
"What we all want from a love story...Don't miss it!"
– *In Print*

To Take This Lord (Brides of Bath, Book 4)
(originally titled *An Improper Proposal*)
"Bolen does a wonderful job building simmering sexual tension between her opinionated, outspoken heroine and deliciously tortured, conflicted hero." – *Booklist of the American Library Association*

My Lord Wicked
Winner, International Digital Award for Best Historical Novel of 2011.

With His Lady's Assistance (Regent Mysteries, Book 1)
"A delightful Regency romance with a clever and personable heroine matched with a humble, but intelligent hero. The mystery is nicely done, the romance is enchanting and the secondary characters are enjoyable." – *RT Book Reviews*

Finalist for International Digital Award for Best Historical Novel of 2011.

A Duke Deceived
"*A Duke Deceived* is a gem. If you're a Georgette Heyer fan, if you enjoy the Regency period, if you like a genuinely sensuous love story, pick up this first novel by Cheryl Bolen." – *Happily Ever After*

Books by Cheryl Bolen

Regency Romance

Brazen Brides Series
   Counterfeit Countess (Book 1)
   His Golden Ring (Book 2)
   Oh What A (Wedding) Night (Book 3)
   Marriage of Inconvenience (Book 4)

House of Haverstock Series
   Lady by Chance (Book 1)
   Duchess by Mistake (Book2)
   Countess by Coincidence (Book 3)

The Brides of Bath Series:
   The Bride Wore Blue (Book 1)
   With His Ring (Book 2)
   The Bride's Secret (Book 3)
   To Take This Lord (Book 4)
   Love in the Library (Book 5)
   A Christmas in Bath (Book 6)

The Regent Mysteries Series:
   With His Lady's Assistance (Book 1)
   A Most Discreet Inquiry (Book 2)
   The Theft Before Christmas (Book 3)
   An Egyptian Affair (Book 4)

The Earl's Bargain
My Lord Wicked
His Lordship's Vow
A Duke Deceived

Novellas:
Christmas Brides (3 Regency Novellas)
Only You

Inspirational Regency Romance
Marriage of Inconvenience

Romantic Suspense
Texas Heroines in Peril Series:
    Protecting Britannia
    Capitol Offense
    A Cry in the Night
    Murder at Veranda House

Falling for Frederick

American Historical Romance
A Summer to Remember (3 American Historical Romances)

World War II Romance
It Had to be You

ONLY YOU

CHERYL BOLEN

$\mathscr{P}$rologue

(The Lore of the Lucius Ring)

By Kathryn Le Veque

128 A.D.
The Junii Villa, 8 miles northwest of Rome

It was a strong breeze that swept off the Tyrrenhian Sea, a breeze that was a breath from the gods, from Poseidon as he bellowed angrily at the land which he could not dominate. This summer season had been unusually warm and the sea breezes reflected that unnatural heat. The locals said that it was because Hades had left the gates of hell open and what they were experiencing was the great belches of infernal fire, but Theodosia dismissed the native dramatics as she usually did. Moreover, she had no time for such things. These days, she had little time for anything other than her own grief.

On the placid morning, Theodosia sat upon a cushioned chair in the *peristylium*, a garden area that was towards the rear of her parents' villa outside of Rome. It was a villa that had been in her family for generations, as her family, the Junii, were long-established nobility among the patrician society of Rome. Along with respect and wealth came privilege, and Theodosia's entire life had been one of advantage and pleasure, and when it came time for her to marry, her father (much the slave to his daughter's wishes), allowed her to select her own husband. Select she did, a young and dashing Roman officer from a good family named Lucius Maximus Aentillius.

Lucius.

The mere name entering her mind used to bring torrents of tears, ever since the letter from the governor of Londinium, addressed to her father, had been received those six months ago. *It is my sincerest regret to inform you that the Twentieth Victorious Valerian Legion was discovered to be overrun upon the great Vallum Aelium. All within the legion were lost.*

Lost....

Now, Theodosia pretended to be numb to the mention of her husband's name because her constant tears frightened her young daughter. *Lucius' daughter.* Whenever she looked into that little face, she saw her husband within in the depths; dark and curly hair, hazel eyes... all of this was Lucius. Mostly, she cried for the child that would never know her father and for the father who never knew he had a child. These days, Theodosia cried many tears for many reasons.

She also cried for herself.

Twenty-three years of age was quite early to be widowed, but that was the position she found herself in. Her family, as well-connected as they were, and with her father being a senator, she knew she would not be able to remain a widow much longer. Already, her father's friend, Proculus Tarquinius Geganius, was filling her father's ear with a stew of poisonous suggestions that would see his son, Marcus, married to Theodosia. Marcus didn't like girl-children, however, so Theodosia's young daughter, Lucia, would have to remain with her grandparents. In spite of the girl-child, however, Marcus was willing to marry the beautiful Theodosia.

Theodosia, however, was unwilling to marry him. Her life, void of joy and cast into a sea of turmoil those six months ago, was threatening to become worse with the axe of marriage hanging over her head. Despair and sorrow were her constant companions. If her parents had anything to say about it, she would marry Marcus and little Lucia would no longer be welcome to live with her mother, but Theodosia would not let that happen.

Above all else, she and Lucia would remain together.

On this warm morning, Theodosia watched Lucia play in the pond in the middle of the *peristylium,* her thoughts lingering on the day she and Lucius had met. It had happened along the sea shore where she had been walking along with friends and collecting lovely shells. Lucius and some of his cohorts had rowed onto the sand from a Roman warship that had been anchored off shore, invading their shell-gathering, but no one seemed to mind at that point. Theodosia and her friends had been laughing, enjoying life and enjoying the sun, when six brawny soldiers disembarked from their cog.

It was a moment that changed Theodosia's life forever.

The soldiers were quite interested in the women along the beach, but Theodosia's friends fled, leaving Theodosia standing on the beach with her apron full of sea shells. Realizing she was alone, she had tried to flee but the sea shells had fallen to the sand and the next she realized, Lucius was helping her pick them all up. She gazed into the man's gentle, warm eyes and she was lost.

A brief courtship followed in the usual fashion except she discovered her lover to be quite prolific with prose – Lucius would write her poetry, in secret of course, because if his cohorts in the legion caught wind of the fact that Lucius would write songs of love and beauty, he might have been laughed at. But, oh, the prose! The beauty of his words! And the last line, in anything he wrote her, was always the same:

Cum cogitationes solum de uobis. With dreams only of you.

Words that had such great meaning to them, in fact, that Lucius had them inscribed on the wedding ring he gave her. It was a family ring that had come through Lucius' very wealthy mother whose family had descended from the Greek gods centuries before. It was said that Silvia's family was half-divine, descended from Mars, and when Lucius gave Theodosia his mother's family ring, he told her that the ring had come from Aphrodite herself. The ring, a very dark gold with a crimson-colored ruby, appeared old enough to have perhaps truly been forged by the gods.

But it was a beautiful ring of great sentimental value. With her parents' permission, Theodosia and Lucius had been married a scant six weeks later and at the reception following their wedding, Lucius' mother, the elegant Lady Silvia, had pulled Theodosia aside. Although the woman had been gracious and affectionate, her attention was not on Theodosia – it had been on the ring.

As I have no daughters, I asked my son to give you this ring meant from my family, she had said. As you wear it upon your finger, I must tell you the legend behind it. Now the ring is a part of you and you are a part of it, and you must pass it down to your daughter, and your daughter must pass it to her daughter. It has been in my family for centuries; some say it was worn by Aphrodite herself. The ring possesses the greatest power of love and when the owner of the ring knows true love, the stone will turn crimson. But if owner of the ring fails to find true love before she has seen twenty-five summers, the stone will turn to dark ember and the owner shall be alone for eternity.

Theodosia had looked at the ring and it was indeed a lovely crimson color. Puzzled, she had spoken freely. *The stone is crimson upon my finger,* she had said, *but I fear you have gifted me with a generous burden. I fear to tell any daughter I may have that if she does not know love by her twenty-fifth summer, then she shall be an old maid.*

Silvia had laughed. *You needn't worry,* she had said. *Any daughter you and my son will have will surely be beautiful and know love.*

Theodosia still wasn't convinced. *Have you ever seen it actually turn to ember?*

Silvia lost some of her humor. *Once,* she had said, *on my spinster aunt. The stone was black and she died old and alone. But before she died, she gave it to me and I soon wed Lucius' father. The stone turned crimson and has been crimson ever since.*

Even now, in the sunshine of her parent's

peristylium, Theodosia recalled that conversation and looked at the ring upon her slender finger, which had turned darker shades since the missive from Londinium those months ago. It wasn't exactly a dark ember color, but it was no longer the rich, red crimson it used to be. Odd how she hadn't noticed that before. The ring, before her eyes, was darkening.

Curious as to the changing color of the ring, Theodosia thought on her age; *I have seen twenty-three summers.* Only two more years to find love again or the ring would darken for the rest of her lifetime. What if what Lady Silvia said was true? What if she would never love again if she did not find it in the next two years?

But her thoughts quickly settled; she had loved once before. She and Lucius had shared a love that mortal men could only dream of. She didn't want to find love again; she wanted to remember Lucius forever as her one and only true love. She didn't want another man's touch to erase that memory.

If the ring turned to black, so be it.

"A beautiful morning, my glory."

Theodosia was rocked from her thoughts of the ring by her father, who came up behind her and kissed her on the head. She covered the ring on her finger, putting her hand over it, as she forced a smile at her father.

"Good morn to you as well," she said

politely. "Where is mother?"

Tiberius Junius Brutus threw a thumb back in the direction of the *cucina*, or kitchen. "There is some crisis regarding a roasting pig, I think," he said, pulling up a chair. "The truth is that I do not know. I try not to involve myself in your mother's affairs because she will pinch me."

Theodosia giggled. "Pinch her in return."

Tiberius shook his head. "Then she will strike me," he said with fear, watching his daughter laugh. "Nay, daughter; I will remain happily out of your mother's affairs. I have come to see you and Lucia this morning."

Theodosia looked over at her daughter, now picking some of her mother's precious pink flowers.

"Lucia!" she called. "Do not pick those flowers!"

The little girl looked up at her mother, grinned, and moved on to the next bush to pick those flowers. Theodosia sighed.

"She is so much like her father," she said softly. "She knows that her smile will ease everything with me. I cannot become angry when she smiles."

Tiberius laughed softly. "Nor can I," he said, tapping his daughter affectionately on the arm. "When you were young, it was the same way with you. I could deny you nothing when you smiled at me."

Theodosia looked at her beloved father,

smiling at the man. "Does it still work?"

He grunted and looked away, aware of her attempt at manipulation. "More than likely."

She chuckled, turning her attention back to her daughter. "That is good to know."

Tiberius cleared his throat again, eyeing his granddaughter as she ripped yellow posies off the vine before returning his gaze to his daughter. His focus lingered on her, his titian-haired daughter that he loved so much. Her heartbreak had been his heartbreak but, as a father, he had the ability to see the bigger picture in her life. He knew she was still grieving for Lucius but to allow her to wallow in that anguish forever would not be a good thing. Theodosia deserved better things in life that to weep over a lost love.

"You seem happier these days, Theo," he ventured. "You are at least smiling again."

Theodosia knew what he meant and the familiar pangs of grief began to come over her again. "Sometimes," she said. "It comes and goes."

Tiberius continued to watch her, noting the expressions of pain upon her face. "It does not have to be like this forever," he said softly. "The time will come again when you are happy. Sometimes the best thing to do is to find another source of happiness."

Theodosia rolled her eyes and stood up. "I do not want to find another source of happiness, Father," she said firmly. "If you are going to bring up Proculus and his pompous son, do not bother. I will not marry Marcus. He means to separate me from my child and I will not have it. It is barbaric."

Tiberius remained calm as his daughter's ire rose. "He is a man who has never been married," he said evenly. "He does not understand the attachment between a mother and her child. I am sure that in time he will come to understand it. He is not an unreasonable man; in fact, he has a very bright future ahead of him. Some say he is to be the next proconsul of Byzantium. He is in much favor with Caesar. You could be his wife, Theodosia, and command much wealth and power. Does this not appeal to you?"

Theodosia was looking at her political-savvy father in horror; she knew the man saw her match to Marcus as a great political marriage that would bring both families prestige. But she wanted no part of it.

"And I must sacrifice my child in order to attain it?" she asked, aghast. Then, she shook her head firmly. "Nay, Father; I will not sacrifice Lucia simply to gain a new husband. I do not *want* a new husband. I thought you understood this."

Tiberius understood it all too well, but he also understand that he, as Theodosia's father, knew what was best for her. He and his wife had been given over to many long discussions about their daughter's future and

Theodosia's mother was also in agreement. They had to do what was best for their child, whether or not she realized it. Lucius was dead and he was never coming back. Theodosia, with or without Lucia, had to move on. But the difficulty would be in the doing.

"Theo," Tiberius said quietly as he rose from his chair. Theodosia was facing the small fish pond in the *peristylium,* refusing to look at him. When he realized she wasn't going to turn around to face him, he cleared his throat softly. "I understand that you are still grieving for Lucius. I understand that you loved the man. But you must understand that life goes on without him. Lucius is dead, Theo; he has been dead for years as far as we know. You have therefore been a widow for at least that long. Will you waste your life lingering in the past, over a love that grew cold years ago? You are more intelligent than that. You were always given free choice in all matters but I find that at this time, I must make your decisions for you since you choose to linger in the darkness. I told Marcus that you would marry him. The contract has been sealed. Tomorrow, Marcus will come for you and you will go with him. You must trust me in this matter, Theodosia. I know what is best for you."

Theodosia had been staring at the fish pond through his speech until he mentioned

Marcus and the marriage. Realizing what her father had done, she looked at the man in outrage.

"You had no right!" she hissed. "No right at all!"

Tiberius would not be sucked into her argument. He turned away. "As your father and the man who provides your food and clothing, I have every right," he told her sternly. "I am sorry if this angers you, Theo, but you will thank me one day. This is what is best for you. Lucia will remain here with your mother and I until such time as Marcus will allow her into his household. She will be happy here, I swear it."

Tiberius was walking away, as he often did with face with enraged or emotional females. Theodosia knew it would do no good to scream at him for it would only make him angry. It would only drive him away to the point where he would lock himself in his room and refuse to come out. Nay, arguing with the man would not bring about his change of mind. Once his mind was set, it was purely stone.

Tears filling her eyes, Theodosia watched her father disappear into the villa, no doubt to inform Theodosia's mother what he had done. *She probably already knows*, Theodosia thought bitterly. She was quite certain they had both had a hand in this because she was also quite certain that her father had tried to deliver this news to her more than once over the past few days but she was in no frame of mind to listen to him. But today, he could no longer delay, especially if Marcus was expecting her on the morrow. Was it really possible?

Oh, God... Marcus...!

Theodosia could not go to him; she *would* not go to him. She would not leave her daughter behind. That being the case, she would either have to fight the man off or run away from him. She chose to run; there was nothing left for her here, anyway, not with Lucius gone. In fact, this entire place reminded her of him, reminded her of the man she had loved and lost. She had to go somewhere else and start anew, a place where there were no memories of Lucius and where overbearing buffoons like Marcus weren't breathing down her neck.

She had to get away.

Lucia was still picking yellow flowers off the vine as her mother came to her and gently led her away. Into the dark, well-furnished villa they went, heading to the *cubiculum* they shared, the one that Theodosia had shared with Lucius before he'd left for Britannica. The chamber was small but well-appointed with a comfortable larger bed and then a smaller one in the corner for Lucia.

Once inside the chamber, Theodosia shut the door and bolted it. The only light and air came from a narrow window up near the ceiling, a window that faced inward to the atrium of the home. On the second floor of the villa as they were, the walls of the chamber were painted beautiful reds and yellows, with a woodland scene against the outer wall.

Lucius had once taken a reed brush and, with black paint he'd taken from the household slaves that worked the maintenance on the villa, painted a giant penis on every animal in the woodland scene. The enormous phalluses were still there and gave Theodosia cause to smile every time she saw them. They reminded her of Lucius and his sense of humor, of the man who could be so loving and yet so naughty at times. She loved that about him. They risqué paintings brought a smile to her lips even now.

So she stood there a moment, grinning at her husband's sense of humor, drinking in the sight to tuck back into her memory for days when she was feeling particularly lonely. She could lose herself in thoughts of Lucius so easily here but she eventually shook them off. She had a job to do. Opening the large chest where clothes and other possessions were kept, she removed a large satchel made from leather and fabric. Quickly, she went to work.

As Theodosia hurriedly packed, Lucia found her poppets and sat upon her little bed, paying with her dolls and the flowers she had picked. At one point, Theodosia's mother knocked on her door, wanting to speak with her, but Theodosia chased her away. She didn't want to speak with her mother. She knew the woman supported her husband's decision to marry off their daughter so she had no desire to speak with her. She had no desire to speak with the woman who would so greedily accept Lucia to raise as her own.

So Theodosia's mother eventually wandered away, distraught, but Theodosia didn't pay the woman any mind. She continued packing her bag, stuffing it with clothing they would need and valuables to sell, including every piece of jewelry her father had ever given her. They were expensive pieces and would bring a goodly sum. Theodosia knew she would need the money.

As she bustled about in her chamber, collecting things of value, she passed by her writing desk and accidentally bumped into it. Pieces of vellum fell to the floor and as she picked them up, her attention was focused on one particular sheet on the top.

My fingers brush the sky; I see your face in the clouds.
In white mist, your smile fills my soul,
My heart has wings!
Upon the breath from the sea, I hear you call

to me,
   Ever, Theodosia, ever my love!
   For separation cannot deny the bonds of our
passionate hearts.

With a sigh, Theodosia slowed in her packing as she read the poem, twice. Lucius had been known to write copious amounts of poetry to her and she, in turn, had learned to write it to him. But that had stopped the moment the missive had come from Londinium. She never wanted to write poetry ever again, for it was something only meant for Lucius. Looking at her words upon the vellum, words she'd hoped to give to Lucius someday, she missed the man all the more. It made her realize that running away was the right thing to do. She would not be separated from the child of the man who instilled such love within her breast. For him, still, her heart had wings and it always would.

She renewed her packing with a sense of urgency now, stronger than before. Her next order of business was to dress her daughter appropriately for travel and she bundled the child up in loosely fitting clothing. Putting a little cap on her head to conceal her dark curls, she dressed appropriately herself in durable traveling clothing. Her dark red hair, so shiny and lovely, was wrapped up in a scarf to conceal it. Dressed and packed, she fed her child the remnants of the fruit and bread and cheese that had been left over from a mid-morning meal and waited for the sun to set.

There was a reason she wanted to wait until sundown; she knew her parents would be taking their naps before the evening meal and the villa would be quiet and still for the most part. Opening her chamber door as the sunlight on the walls turned shades of pink and gold, she slipped from her chamber and down the stairs that led to the *vestibulum*, or entry, as her chamber was very close to it.

There were a few servants about but they didn't notice her as she slipped out into the olive grove that was immediately outside, using the darkened trees with their dark green leaves so shield her flight. As the night birds began to forage overhead and the sea breeze blew cool and damp, Theodosia and Lucia slipped away from *Villa Junii,* making their way to the inland road that would lead to the north.

It was a long flight into the night that did not stop even when the sun rose again. It was well into the next day when Theodosia, carrying the sleeping Lucia on her shoulder as she trudged down the tree-lined road, heard the sounds of a wagon behind her. Fearful it might be her father, for she had already evaded his patrols twice, she slipped off the road and allowed the cart to pass, noting it was a lone man with an empty cart.

The wagon bed was covered in chaff.

Hopeful that she might have found a ride to the mountainous interior region where she hoped to find shelter, she came out of her hiding place and began to walk quickly after the cart. She could only pray the man at the reins was a kind and moral soul. At this point she didn't much care because her exhaustion and hunger had the better of her. She needed rest and food badly, overriding her common sense.

"Sir?" she called after him. "*Sir?*"

The man in the cart, hearing the voice behind him, turned around to the source but kept going. However, when he saw the woman with the small child following him, he came to a halt. Relieved, Theodosia ran up to the wagon bench.

"Good sir," she said, weary and hopeful. "Would you be kind enough to take my child and I with you?"

The man, younger, with handsome and somewhat rugged blond looks, nodded. "Where are you going?"

Theodosia lifted the half-asleep Lucia onto the wagon bench and the man grasped the child so she wouldn't slither away. Theodosia climbed up onto the bench and took Lucia back into her arms, holding the child tightly.

"I... I am going up this road a way," she said, uncertain what to tell the man who seemed to be gazing at her with some interest. "Thank you for your graciousness."

The man clucked softly at the big brown horse, who began to walk again. He eyed Theodosia somewhat, curious about the beautiful woman with the sleeping child. He also noticed the traveling clothes, the bag. "Have you been traveling far?" he asked politely.

Theodosia nodded. "Very far."

"Where are you going?"

Theodosia had no idea what to tell him so she avoided answering. She glanced at the wagon bed, covered in chaff. "Are you a farmer?" she asked.

The man nodded. "My father and I have a large farm near Cesaro," he said. "I go into Rome once a week to sell our produce at the markets. I am just returning."

Theodosia glanced at the man; he had pale blue eyes and very big, muscular hands. "What do you sell?"

"Grain, mostly," he said. "We also have a small vineyard and my father makes wine."

Theodosia was interested in such a life; men and women who worked the land had always fascinated her. *To be so useful,* she thought. She had no idea what it truly meant to be useful, just as she had no idea what it truly meant to run away from her father's home. Already, they had faced some hunger and hardship. She was frightened. But she also felt strangely free.

"Do you do well at the market?" she asked, genuinely curious. "That is to say, are you able to do well enough to feed yourself and your family?"

When he caught her looking at him, he smiled and his eyes crinkled. "I do well enough," he told her. "But it is just my father and me. There are only two mouths to feed."

"No wife?"

"I was married, once, but she died giving birth to my son, who also died."

Theodosia sobered. "I am sorry," she said. "I did not mean to pry."

The man shook his head. "You did not," he said, eyeing her now with more interest than curiosity. "My name is Gaius, by the way."

"I am Theodosia. This is my daughter, Lucia."

"Where are you going, Theodosia? To see your family?"

Theodosia shook her head and looked away. "Nay."

"Your husband, perhaps?"

Again, she shook her head. "My husband is dead."

"And you are running from his cruel family who beats you daily and forces you into slavery?"

Theodosia grinned in spite of her herself. "Nay," she said. "I have been living with my family. My husband's family is all dead."

Gaius was an extraordinarily intelligent

man for being a farmer; in fact he had been schooled in his youth and spent several years in the Roman army, but an ill father and a failing farm had caused him to return home.

Bright as he was, he knew there was much more to Theodosia than she was telling him. She was a stunningly beautiful woman with soft white hands and smooth skin and if he could guess about her, he would say she was a noblewoman. She just had that look about her, regal and elegant. But she was running from something, or someone, and the protective male in him seemed to be taking great interest in her. It probably wasn't healthy for him, for he'd never had good fortune with women, but he couldn't help himself. Something about Theodosia drew him to her.

But she obviously didn't feel the same way about him. She had refused to answer his questions about where she was going so he was coming to suspect that perhaps she didn't even know. She appeared very tired and hungry, and her little girl was exhausted. He was more than likely a fool for being sympathetic to her, but he was.

"If your destination is too far away, my farm is only an hour ahead," he told her casually. "It is getting late. If you would like to rest the night, as our guest, we would be happy to have you and your daughter. In fact, my dog just had a litter of puppies your daughter might like to play with. Otherwise, they will be very lonely puppies."

Theodosia looked at the man, shocked by his offer. *Do not agree!* She told herself, suspicious of the Gaius' ulterior motive. But the truth was that a night in a safe home with a warm fire was too good to resist. Perhaps it would be the most foolish thing she ever did in her life to accept his invitation, but she found herself quite willing to do it. For her daughter's sake, she had to.

"Well," she said, pretending to be reluctant. "I suppose we could, just for the night, of course. We would be gone by sunrise."

Gaius nodded. "As you wish," he said, eyeing her. "If... if you perhaps need to earn some money for your trip, there are chores about the farm that need to be done. I would pay you for them."

Theodosia looked at him in surprise. "Chores?" she repeated, both disgusted and intrigued. "Like what?"

Gaius grinned at the dismay in her tone, which only proved his theory that she was a noblewoman who did not do manual work. "Milking the goats," he told her. "Sweeping. Cooking. We can always use help if you are looking for a job."

A job. Theodosia had to admit that she was very interested. It would be some place for her and Lucia to stay, to be together, and for her to earn a living even though she'd never earned a living in her life. Still, it might be the opportunity she needed. She tried not to seem too eager about it.

"We can discuss it, I suppose," she said. "But you should know I have never milked a goat in my life."

He grinned, glancing at her lily-white hands. "Is that so?" he said, somewhat wryly. "I would never have guessed. It is easy to learn."

"Is it?"

"I can will teach you."

"I cannot cook, either."

"I can teach you that, too."

Theodosia thought, perhaps, that it all sounded too good to be true. Were the gods sending her a sign or was Hades providing a trap for being a disobedient daughter? She couldn't be sure, but she was attracted to Gaius' offer. It was a struggle not to become excited about it.

"But my daughter must stay with me," she said. "You do not mind a child about?"

Gaius shook his head. "My father always wanted a grandchild. He will like having her about."

Theodosia didn't know what to say; she was coming to think that, indeed, the gods knew of her plight and had brought Gaius into her life at precisely the correct time. Was it even possible that all of this could be true? She would soon find out.

Gaius and his father, Agrippus, lived like two bachelors on a very large farm. There was plenty of work to be done and Theodosia wasn't afraid to learn. In fact, she rather liked it. Gaius taught her to cook and to milk goats, to press wine and make flour. Theodosia learned quickly. She soon came to love her new life and, in time, love for Gaius bloomed as well. A truly good-hearted man who readily accepted Lucia, Theodosia knew that the decision to leave her parents' home had been the best decision she had ever made. She knew that Lucius would have approved.

With the introduction of Gaius, the ring that Lucius had given her those years ago once again turned a deep, rich crimson and would remain so until the day Theodosia passed it on to Lucia on the day of her eighteenth birthday. Fortunately for Lucia, the ring would turn crimson two years later at the introduction of a certain young soldier who happened to cross her path.

The ring of Lucius' family, the ring of true love or of lost love, continued to live on through the ages, passed down from Lucia to her daughter, and from her daughter onward. The story of the ring was also passed along with it, an oral tradition for the female members of the family, and through the centuries, the eldest daughter of each generation would hold great hope that the ring would turn crimson for her. Somewhere along the line, it was said that if one spoke the words inscribed upon the ring, *with dreams only of you*, that a lover would appear within a fortnight. Many a young woman believed in those words. Many a young woman was rewarded for that belief.

But a few were not. No one could be sure why those spellbound words sometimes worked or sometimes didn't, or why love would turn the stone to crimson and heartache would turn it to black, but it didn't really matter. It was a glorious tradition within the females of the family and the mystery of the crimson-stoned ring continued to brand Theodosia's descendants with its particular kind of magic.

The lore of the Lucius Ring lived on.

$\mathcal{C}$hapter 1

London, 1788

Annie slammed shut the dressing table drawer. "I am going to kill her!"

The sudden movement and shrill words sent the cat in her lap into a hissing, leaping frenzy, which caused Annie's maid to drop the comb which in turn dislodged Annie's artfully arranged hair.

Annie raced from her bedchamber and along the corridor to her sister's chamber, Eliza and a still-angry Flufferness trailing after her.

"What has yer sister gone and done now? Can ye not wait until I finish dressing yer hair, milady?" Eliza asked.

Lady Annia—Annie—Childe shook her head. "The Thief has stolen my amethyst bracelet." She paused in front of her sister's bedchamber door only long enough to angrily bang it open and charged in like a lancer in battle.

Fanny was peering into her looking glass, a satisfied expression on her face. She was dressed to perfection in fine pink silk, embroidered satin slippers, and a sparkling bracelet. *My bracelet*, Annie thought.

Unlike her now-livid twin, Fanny's lightly powdered hair was styled in the latest fashion, piled elegantly upon her head. Her impeccable appearance was polished off with a strategically placed patch on her left cheek.

Annie squinted as she peered at her sister's cheeks. *Mama's French rouge*! Of course, Fanny, with her larcenous persuasion, had no compunction about helping herself to their mother's rouge.

Anyone observing Annie's twin would never take so angelic looking a girl for a thief.

The two sisters' eyes met. Annie's glare indicated she *was* capable of fratricide. For a fraction of a second, fear registered in Fanny's eyes, then she turned up her nose and spoke haughtily. "Pray, why do you look at me as if I'd just escaped from Bedlam?"

"Not Bedlam," Annie hissed. "Newgate. Can the daughter of an earl be hanged as a thief?"

Fanny rolled her eyes. "If this is about your Rousseau, I can explain. I wanted to read just one passage so I could converse intelligently with Mr. Douglass, then I planned to return it."

Annie's anger singed. "You took my Rousseau too? Have I not told you a thousand times to ask permission before helping yourself to property that is *not* yours?"

"It was only going to be for an hour or two."

Annie folded her arms across the lace-trimmed bodice of her dress and glared at Fanny from beneath lowered brows. "A perfect example of your shallowness. You're too lazy to read the whole of any book which will enrich your mind. You're a cheat. And a thief."

"I am not a thief!" Fanny's protest was even louder than Annie's accusation.

"You are too! Yesterday it was my diamond hair combs. Today it's my amethyst bracelet."

"So that's what this is about? You're angry because I *borrowed* you bracelet?"

"Stole it. Why can you not wear your diamond one? I need mine tonight."

Flufferness leapt onto Fanny's dressing table, scattering perfume bottles and jewelry, and settled her paws in Lady Tolworth's rouge pot.

"Get your wretched animal out of here!"

Annie crossed the chamber and lifted her cat. "How dare you order me—or my cat—about." She tried to give the animal a cuddle, but the contrary feline wanted no part of it. "And my cat has a name."

The door to Fanny's chamber burst open, and there stood Lady Tolworth. "I could hear you two screeching like banshees. What is it now?" She scowled at Annie but did not pause for a response. "I declare, I never heard of sisters arguing like the two of you. And to think, you're twins! You may look exactly the same—when . . ." Lady Tolworth paused once more to scowl at Annie, " . . .when Annie deigns to make herself presentable—but never were two sisters more opposed in nature." Another scowl was directed at Annie. "I don't know why you cannot be more like Fanny." Her gaze went to the messy dressing table. "Whatever happened here?"

Fanny frowned. "Annie's cat."

Lady Tolworth pulled the bell for the butler.

Annie seethed. "I have no desire to be a thief. Even if that thief displays a pretty countenance."

Lady Tolworth's eyes narrowed. "I will not permit you to call your sister a thief."

Annie looked to her maid for support, but Eliza was quietly exiting Fanny's bedchamber. *Coward.*

When the butler came, her ladyship said, "Pray, Dobbs, do remove this disobedient cat from *both* of my daughters' bedchambers."

Pouting, Annie attempted to hug her cat before the poor thing was taken to the dungeon, but Fluffferness was in no mood for such a display.

Unbeknownst to Annie, the cat's paw left a rouge stamp upon her left cheek.

Fanny moved to their mother, smiling and joining arms. "We must go down to dinner. I am massively anxious to meet the Duke of Axminster."

"Indeed," Lady Tolworth said, "What a splendid match he would be for you, dearest. He's not only handsome and very, very wealthy, but he's a duke!" She patted Fanny's hand, then turned back to Annie. "Is that the best Eliza could do with your hair?" Not allowing a response, she sighed and continued. "You must come as you are. It would be epically rude to be late at one's own house with so distinguished a guest."

Annie followed behind. "I hope the duke falls in love with Fanny. I can't be rid of The Thief too soon."

"You know you would miss her."

In this, Mama was correct.

* * *

Alexander Halsey, the Duke of Axminster, did not attend assemblies. He avoided Ranelagh pleasure gardens as consistently as he boycotted balls. To preserve his ducal peace, he made it a general rule that he never attended functions where matchmaking mamas and unwed damsels would contrive to snare him with their beauty, accomplishments, and dazzling wit. He'd yet to meet a lady in whom that trio of attributes combined.

He had made an exception tonight.

He had agreed to dine with Lord Tolworth even knowing the earl was father to two reputed beauties his countess was anxious to marry off—especially to a duke.

Dining with the man Alex considered the wisest and most respected member of the House of Lords was worth sitting through a dinner in which Lady Tolworth would sing the praises of her twin girls. Alex fully expected to be informed that the beauties could sing like nightingales. That the Childe girls could dance with the grace of a swan was also sure to be affirmed. It would not surprise him if Lady Tolworth just happened to mention that her accomplished daughters presided over a salon brimming with besotted admirers every day they were in the Capital.

Once his coachman knocked upon the Tolworth's door and announced his master, the duke was greeted in a most peculiar manner. The butler, who was holding a fat cat, directed that animal's posterior toward Alex's face. A most singular occurrence, to be sure.

That servant showed Alex to the drawing room. A short time later Lady Tolworth and her twins entered the chamber, and he stood. His quick glance confirmed the twins were possibly identical, slender, and taller than average. Pretty, too. As a gentleman, he directed his attentions on their mother. "Ah, Lady Tolworth, I thought for a moment Lord Tolworth must have three daughters," Alex flattered when the host presented his wife.

"Your grace is far too kind." Her lashes lowered, then her glance lifted to the daughter nearest her. "Allow me to present to you my daughter, Lady Fannia."

There was no coy dropping of lashes with this miss. She flashed a brilliant smile upon him as she curtsied, never removing her sparkling gaze from his. "I cannot deny what a pleasure it is to meet you, your grace. Though you never attend assemblies, we've heard much about you. How gratifying it is to finally make your acquaintance."

He was immediately struck over her face. It was, quite possibly, the finest bone structure he'd ever beheld. Her cheekbones were high, the light brown brows perfectly arched, her aquiline nose sheer perfection, and her full mouth as flawless as the rest of the face. There was a delicacy about her fair colouring and slender appearance that was at odds with the confidence she exuded.

"And it's a pleasure to meet the Childe sisters." He eyed the second one. Then he quickly looked back at Lady Fannia to confirm that they were indeed twins. He felt certain they were, but this second one seemed vastly different. She possessed the same remarkable face, but instead of a discreet patch of dark velvet as Lady Fannia wore, this sister's cheek was adorned with a red cat's paw. How singular. There was also the matter of this twin's hair. It looked as if she had just climbed from her bed, and unlike her sister, she wore no jewelry.

Lord Tolworth stepped up and introduced this sister. "Your grace, it is my pleasure to present my daughter Lady Annia to you. It is the custom in my wife's family to give the daughters old Roman names, in case you were wondering. We call the twins Annie and Fanny."

"Ah, the rhyming Childes," Alex quipped.

"Indeed," Lord Tolworth said.

The much more shy Lady Annia stepped forward, but only barely met his gaze before lowering her lashes and dipping into a curtsy. Alex would wager this sister, unlike her mother, did not avert her gaze from coyness. She appeared genuinely reticent. Even if she bore a cat's paw upon her very pretty cheek.

"I am charmed," Alex said to the more modest twin.

She looked up at him and smiled. "I look forward to hearing you discuss Parliament."

Of the hundreds of maidens he'd met, this was the first who admitted to an interest in politics. How singular.

"Watch out, your grace, or my Annie will talk your head off about Parliament." Under his breath, Lord Tolworth mumbled, "Should have been a son." He sighed. "Dinner awaits. If you would be so kind, your grace, as to lead Lady Tolworth into the dining room."

As Alex expected, a Childe sister sat at each side of him, and their mother was close enough to directly address him. They were the only three ladies at the gathering. Lord Tolworth had invited several leading members of both houses of Parliament.

Alex was in his element when surrounded by leaders of the government. He could not wait until dinner was finished, the women left, and the men could drink port and discuss politics.

Halfway through the soup, Lady Tolworth claimed his attention. "Do you play at the pianoforte, your grace?"

Alex shrugged. "I can, but it's not something I pursue."

Not to be deterred, Lady Tolworth said, "A music lover, to be sure. Wait until you hear our Fanny sing. I shouldn't like to boast, but we are told she sings like a nightingale. You shall have to judge for yourself, your grace."

"I shall look forward to it." He smiled at Lady Fannia, then turned to the other sister, the disheveled one. "And do you sing, Lady Annia?"

She shrugged. "Not as beautifully as Fanny."

Lady Tolworth frowned. "Annie disdains many of the feminine pursuits. While our Fanny dances as smoothly as a swan gliding across a pond, Annie abhors dancing and assemblies."

He smiled to himself. They had not finished the first course and already the twins' proud mother had fulfilled two of his prophecies.

"Then it appears Lady Annia and I have much in common," he said.

Now the shy sister eyed him. Not as boldly as her sister continued to do but as one would gaze upon a long-standing acquaintance. "I believe we do, your grace. I am a student of political philosophy, and from what I've read in the newspapers, you are too."

Now he gave her his full attention. He did not even notice how askew her hair was. "Do not tell me you've read Paine?"

"Of course I have."

He smiled. "Then your father's Whig sympathies have passed to this daughter?"

"Even were he not my father, I would greatly admire my sire."

"Have you met Charles James Fox?"

She frowned. "Would that I had. Papa generally meets with him at Brooks." She brightened. "I *have* been privileged to hear Mr. Fox speak in the House of Commons. His breadth of knowledge is amazing."

"I agree, Lady Annia. Allow me to say you're the only lady I know who sits in the galleries."

"There is no place I would rather be—at least when a great orator is scheduled to speak."

"Another matter in which we are in perfect agreement."

Lady Tolworth cleared her throat and directed her attention at the duke. "Do you enjoy paying morning calls, your grace?"

"No. It's not something I enjoy."

"A pity," the elder lady said. "Our salon is filled every day with gentlemen, but our Fanny has yet to meet a man worthy of one with all her attributes."

Three, he thought.

He eyed his hostess. "I would say both ladies possess may fine attributes."

Lady Tolworth glowed. And her lashes lowered.

How he wished he were at the other end of the table where Lord Tolworth was discussing Warren Hastings. The two men's gazes locked. "I warn you, your grace, my Annie will direct all the conversation to civil liberties. I daresay she knows more about the subject than any of my colleagues—and I assure you no topic could bore the other females more."

"I do hate the way my dear Tolworth spends so many evenings away," Lady Tolworth said. "If the House of Lords is not meeting well into the night—which is an exceedingly common occurrence—he's off at Brooks with the same group of men—along with the Whigs from the House of Commons." She sighed. "I worry about him eating properly. The dear gets so caught up in his passion for Parliament he forgets to eat."

Lady Annia peered at him. "Even after a quarter of a century, my mother is still besotted over Papa."

Lady Tolworth looked at the large ruby ring upon her right hand. "See. The stone's still red."

He was puzzled. Why wouldn't a ruby be red? And what did that have to do with the longevity of her love?

Lady Fannia explained. "Mama's ring that reportedly dates to Roman times has been passed down the female branch of her family for hundreds of years. If the wearer loves and is loved in return, the stone stays red. It changes colours—to black—when the lady has no love. The ring will come to me."

"Not necessarily," Lady Annia interjected.

Lady Fannia stiffened. "I *am* the oldest."

"You are not!" the other sister contradicted.

"Girls!" their mother admonished. "No one knows which of you was born first—owing to the incompetence of that nurse. Even in my pitiable state of infirmity on the day of your birth, I ordered that foolish nurse to tie a pink ribbon on the wrist of the girl who came first, but the silly woman forgot."

"Nevertheless," Lady Fannia said, "I know I am the oldest."

Lady Annia glared. "You can't possibly know that."

"I do too. I am a half inch taller."

"Forgive me, dear sister, but that's the most imbecilic thing I've ever heard. Height is *not* an indication of age."

Alex was inclined to agree.

Their mother sighed. "Girls!"

"I'm assuming the ring goes to the eldest sister?" he said, looking from one to the other.

"Since we don't know which of us is the eldest," the smarter twin said, "it's best that the ring goes to the first of us who finds a true love."

"I agree," Lady Tolworth said, beaming at Lady Fannia.

That daughter straightened up and favored him with a dazzling smile. "That will be me, I am sure," Lady Fannia said.

"It certainly will," Lady Annia agreed, "if eagerness to entrap a husband is an indicator." Then the lady must have realized how uncharitable that comment sounded for she quickly amended it. "Forgive me, Fanny. What I meant was that the ring will likely go to you because you have a stronger desire than I to marry." Her voice softened. "I truly hope you find your heart's desire."

Lady Fannia smiled upon him.

She was exquisite. "A lovely lady like you is sure to capture the heart of a worthy man."

Her lashes lowered.

* * *

Tonight was every bit as mortifying as the time her drawers fell to the ground as she entered the drawing room filled with nosegay-bearing suitors. Annie still shuddered at the memory.

Even that day, though, she'd been dressed prettily with perfectly coiffed hair—not that any man in that chamber would have noticed. All eyes had latched on to those drawers littering the Aubusson carpet like ink splotches on a white gown.

Tonight's embarrassment almost eclipsed that debacle. As she had entered the dining chamber, she'd caught a glimpse of herself in the looking glass. What the devil was that bright red thing on her cheek? It looked like . . . like a paw print! Oh dear, Flufferness must have dipped her paws into Mama's rouge pot!

Annie inwardly groaned. All this humiliation was Fanny's fault. Eliza would have finished her hair had not Fanny stolen Annie's bracelet, necessitating the trip to Fanny's room, which distressed the poor sleeping kitty in Annie's lap—not that Flufferness was exactly a kitty.

She wished she had allowed Eliza to finish her hair. She wished she were wearing her amethyst bracelet that so beautifully complemented her lavender gown. She wished she could have looked her best when she met the Duke of Axminster for the first time.

Instead she looked like a madwoman who quite possibly thought herself a cat.

Annie suddenly found herself wishing the duke was not so fine looking. Then, perhaps, Fanny wouldn't have set her cap for him—as she'd so obviously done. One look at him, and

Annie had known why he did not attend assemblies. He would be mobbed by females vying to be duchess to the incredibly handsome Duke of Axminster.

Annie herself—never one to ogle over a man—hadn't been able to remove her gaze from his tall, lithe body. His long limbs were sheathed in gray breeches, and his broad shoulders were encased in a black velvet frockcoat. He eschewed the practice of wearing a wig and merely lightly powdered his dark hair that was bound into a queue that trailed down his back.

In spite of the finery of his clothing, there was a ruggedness about him. Perhaps it was his piercing black eyes beneath the hood of dark brows. Or was it the square cut of his powerful jaw? Whatever it was, the man was compelling.

All the newspaper articles she'd read about his supposedly radical beliefs came rushing back. When he started speaking—speaking of topics upon which she agreed wholeheartedly—she would have felt this man was her destiny, were it not for the fact he was a duke. How could a tall, bony girl like her ever hope to capture the affections of a duke?

There was also the matter of his handsomeness. A handsome duke could easily merit the most beautiful, exalted lady in the land. And that most assuredly was not she. Even if she had been at her best. Which she most certainly was *not* tonight.

Why was it the first time she ever wished to look lovely for a man was the first time she had ever stepped into Society looking so unkempt?

She glared across the table at her twin, who was practically purring over the duke. To her consternation, Annie found herself thinking how prettily her amethyst bracelet complemented Fanny's pink frock. How she longed to swish the claret in her glass onto Fanny's dress! Then her sister could experience some of the humiliation Annie suffered. Because of her.

After realizing how pitiable she looked, Annie determined not to talk to the dukely paragon. Then he would not have to peer at her.

This ploy, however, proved unsuccessful. The man persisted in directing questions at her.

"What, my lady, think you of Jeremy Bentham?" he asked Annie.

She regarded him with a smirk. "What makes you think I've read him?" Of course, she'd read every single word ever penned by the man.

"I would wager my matched bays that you have."

"You're awfully sure of yourself. I suppose such a manner is consistent with being a duke."

He flashed a smile. "Of course, but you've not answered me."

"It pains me to inform you that you're correct," she finally said. "I suppose you're accustomed to always being correct."

"Really, Annie!" their mother chided. "How can you speak so rudely to our esteemed guest?"

"I beg that you not chastise your daughter, Lady Tolworth," he said. "Lady Annia and I are merely engaging in friendly banter. Your daughter is most refreshing."

"Thank you, your grace. I assure you, Lady Annia normally looks much prettier. If you care to see how she usually appears, look at Lady Fannia." Lady Tolworth gazed with pride upon that sister.

The duke's gaze flicked to Fanny, and he gave a quick nod. "Allow me to say how lovely you are, Lady Fannia." He turned to Annie. "And you too, Lady Annia."

Both girls inclined their heads and quietly expressed their gratitude.

Then he once again began addressing Annie, and she was obliged to converse with him—even if it did mean he'd have a greater likelihood of examining her slovenly appearance.

The remainder of the dinner, they never lacked for a topic to discuss. As long as it pertained to politics.

Did she approve of the French path to liberty? Had she read Edmond Burke's newest? Had she ever heard Sheridan's orations in the House of Commons?

That last question launched her into a gush of praise. "I have never heard a more clever man," she answered. "Sheridan is possessed of great wit as well as a very fine voice which has a depth of volume."

"I will own," the duke said, "I would gladly pay a hefty subscription for the privilege of hearing that man speak."

"Pray, your grace," Fanny interrupted, "don't allow my sister to bore you with that incessant talk of politics."

"But my dear Lady Fannia, it's not boring to me," he said.

Fanny's smile froze. "I daresay you read Rousseau."

"Who doesn't?" he responded.

"My sister doesn't."

"That's not true!" Fanny protested.

"Reading a handful of pages is not the same as reading an entire book," Annie said. "And you never read an entire book."

"That's not true!" Because everyone nowadays spouted Rousseau and Voltaire, Fanny knew she could not admit the truth without admitting to an absence of attics.

Annie would not have revealed her sister's shameful secret were it not for the fact the cheating sister had ruined her night.

How Annie wished she looked pretty. She'd never before known a man she wished to find her beautiful. Until tonight.

And she could not have looked worse.

Now the duke began to discuss Rousseau with Fanny. Would he realize how much she was evading answering him? Would he guess by the few questions she addressed to him, that those were the only passages in Rousseau that she could discuss?

Later that night, when the duke went to take his leave, he eyed Annie, then Fanny, then Lady Tolworth. "Will you be home for callers tomorrow?"

Chapter 2

For all of her nineteen years, Annie had always slept like a baby. Nothing had ever deprived her of sleep—not the night before her come-out, nor the exhilarating night after Papa made his maiden speech in the House of Lords, not even that night the gales had resulted in a dozen broken windows at Brentley Manor.

But last night she had hardly slept a wink. She kept picturing those black eyes of the Duke of Axminster regarding her with amusement. She kept remembering every subject they had discussed. When she thought of him paying a call on her house that afternoon, her insides fluttered, and she launched into a mental catalog of every dress she owned. What would she wear? It was vitally important after last night's fiasco that she look as pretty as possible today for she thought she might possibly be falling in love with the duke.

She wasn't sure because she had no basis of comparison. Never before had she been in love. What she was experiencing must be. Only the strongest emotions would elicit such visceral response, and she'd experienced several physical responses to the handsome duke. Her breath had grown short when she'd observed him. Thinking of his coming to her house today sent her heart racing.

She dismissed the green muslin because it did nothing to draw the eye away from her resemblance to a flag pole. The scarlet gave the false impression she possessed a bosom. Which was good. But the colour was perhaps too vibrant for her. Because of her fairness, she thought accentuating the delicacy of her colouring and features would enhance her appeal. Last night's lavender would have been perfect. If she'd had her amethyst bracelet.

By the time cheerful Eliza entered her bedchamber the following morning, Annie had decided which dress she would wear. "I shall need you to see that my powdery blue muslin is freshly ironed."

Eliza drew open the draperies at each of the windows in Anne's corner bedchamber. "Ye'll be needing it this afternoon?"

"Yes."

"It's me favorite of all yer gowns. Ye look like an angel in it."

"Thank you. I hope a certain gentleman agrees."

Eliza's face brightened. "I've never before seen ye care a fiddle what any gent thinks of ye. Who *is* this man?"

"I dare not say his name because I'm so

unworthy of him. He's sure to marry well above me."

"Don't ye *ever* go saying such!" Eliza stood before Annie's bed, gazing at her through narrowed eyes. "There's not a lady in the three kingdoms who's as fine as me Lady Annia Childe. Ye're beautiful and smart and kind. And ye're an earl's daughter with a nice dowry. A man could not want for more."

Annie regarded the former parlor maid she'd elevated to her lady's maid at the time of her presentation two years earlier. Her copper-colored curls sparkling in the morning light, Eliza was ten years Annie's senior but displayed a youthful countenance. What a jewel she had turned out to be! She was possessed of an uncommon flair for styling hair—so beautifully that Fanny begrudgingly admitted her skill surpassed that of her own French maid. "I am most fortunate to have you, dear Eliza."

The door to Annie's chamber opened, and Fanny stood there in her night shift, smiling broadly. "Is not the Duke of Axminster the most handsome man in all of England?"

Annie glared. She knew there was nothing Fanny wouldn't do to snare so lofty a peer. Especially one who was so sinfully handsome. "I daresay you wouldn't say that if he were a mere mister like your Mr. Douglass."

"He's not *my* Mr. Douglass!"

"Mr. Douglass does adore you."

Fanny grimaced. "So declares all of his very bad poetry. And I would too find the Duke of Axminster handsome even if he were a footman."

"There is the fact that you have found the last three footmen to come to Tolworth House exceedingly handsome."

Fanny frowned. "I hardly ever notice footmen. Unless they are handsome." She sighed. "Can you credit it—the duke who never pays calls is coming to see me this afternoon!"

"Us. He's coming to see us. And if the truth be known, it's obvious he prefers me over you."

Fanny returned her glare. "He couldn't possibly. Had you peered into a looking glass last night you would have seen how hideous you looked. I daresay he was just being kind because he took pity on you."

"The man admires a well-informed mind, and that, my dear sister, is something you do *not* possess!"

"Did you not say just before we went downstairs last night that you hoped I *did* marry him? Because I mean to have him."

Annie sighed. "Another matter over which we are now opposed."

"You can't mean that you're going to try to capture him? You've never been interested in men be- - -," Fanny paused, her face collapsing. "You *have* fallen for him!"

"I have, but I doubt a man with all his attributes would be interested in a skinny lady void of a nicely rounded bosom. Make that two skinny ladies."

Fanny came and sat on the edge of Annie's bed. "I prefer the word *slender*. And I don't feel it's such a detriment. Any man with sense should realize that most slender maidens turn into well-shaped women whereas well-shaped maidens turn into fat matrons."

Fanny did not usually converse so sensibly. "True. But we're still hideously tall."

"I do wish we were shorter, but the duke *is* a very tall man."

"And so is Mr. Douglass."

"Mr. Douglass is not a duke."

"But he's as wealthy as a duke."

Fanny shrugged. "Which is why I allow him to court me. It does add to my consequence that the wealthiest man in all of Scotland adores me." Fanny's gaze fanned across the chamber. "Where is that cat of yours?"

Annie frowned. "She's been banished to the dungeon, and it's all your fault."

"Pray tell, how is it my fault?"

"She was so upset when you stole my amethyst bracelet that she disturbed your dressing table, and Mama sent her away as punishment." Annie flicked off the bed coverings, sprang from the bed, and went to sit before her dressing table. "I believe I'll have Eliza start arranging my hair now. I hope to look my best for the duke."

"What will you wear?" Fanny asked.

"I've decided on my powdery blue."

Fanny only barely managed a deflated, "Oh." Then she left the room.

* * *

Shortly after returning to her bedchamber from Mama's sitting room, where the Childe ladies gathered every day at noon, Annie looked for her pale blue dress, but it wasn't there. Moments later Eliza entered her room. "Where did you put my blue dress?"

Brows lowered, Eliza flicked her gaze to her mistress's bed. "I laid it out on yer bed as soon as I ironed it so as not to wrinkle it."

"When?"

"Better than 'alf an hour ago."

Annie's heartbeat pounded with fury as she raced to the corridor. "I really will kill her this time!"

Throwing open the door to Fanny's bedchamber, she eyed Monique. "Where is my sister?"

"Your sister has gone down to greet Monsieur Douglass."

"What was she wearing?" Surely The Thief wouldn't have taken her blue gown.

Monique cowered. "The light blue," she whispered. "She assured me she had your permission to wear it."

"She's not only a thief. She's a liar!" And a cheat, Annie thought, storming back to her own bedchamber. Obviously, Fanny had decided that cheating was permissible in order to win the Duke of Axminster.

Annie vowed to get even.

But what would she wear? The duke would be arriving at any moment. Tears of frustration pricked at her eyes. Her first inclination was to forfeit seeing *Him* today. She had so wished to look lovely—especially after last night. Then she knew her absence would only enable Fanny to gain a stronghold in his affections.

Sad to say, she was not even certain her sister would not try to malign her in order to elevate her own standing with the duke. Such suspicions were most uncharitable, especially since they were likely unwarranted. The twins might say wretched things to one another but never outside their family circle.

But, then, the stakes had never before been so high.

There was nothing for it. Annie would be forced to wear the same lavender dress she'd worn the previous night. None of her other dress could achieve the effect she sought.

After Eliza freshened it and helped Annie dress, she went downstairs where the day's callers were assembling.

When Annie entered the drawing room, a half a dozen gentlemen rose from their elegant French chairs. She only had eyes for one of them. The Duke of Axminster had indeed come! During her sleepless night, she had given a great deal of consideration to the manner in which she should greet him. Should she be coy? Or bold and confident like Fanny? Should she feign disinterest? In the end, she decided she would greet him as she would a close friend.

It was no easy task to appear to be unaffected by his presence when she curtsied before him, and he came to draw her (trembling, she was sure) hand into his. Again, there was amusement in his black eyes when he spoke. "Since Lady Fannia preceded you, I don't have to ask which twin you are. Permit me to say you look even lovelier than you did last night, Lady Annia."

She wondered if he had also told Fanny she was lovely. "It is very kind of you to say so, your grace. Permit me to say how gratified we are to have you once again as our guest."

After she sat down, Mr. Douglass continued reading the sonnet he'd composed in Fanny's honor. Fanny couldn't have looked more queenly had she a huge diamond crown circling her powdered tresses.

Annie thought Mr. Douglass was very dear. He was even taller than the duke and possessed of a fine athletic body, pleasing masculine face, and wore a white wig over his thick red hair. Like the duke, he dressed with excellent taste.

He would make Fanny a good husband.

Her sister thrived under adulation.

"I declare, Mr. Douglass, that is the finest piece you've written yet," Fanny praised when he finished. She took the copy of the poem while furtively looking in the direction of the Duke of Axminster.

"I daresay," Mr. Douglass said, "you'll just add it to your collection."

"I am fortunate, indeed, to have so many . . . . admirers," Fanny said, peering modestly into her lap.

A patch of silence followed. Since that never happened, it must be attributed to the presence of so high-ranking a peer. It was as if none of those gathered knew how to comport themselves in his midst.

"Your grace," Annie finally said, "will have to try to convert Mr. Douglass. He serves as a Tory in the House of Commons."

The two men's eyes locked.

"Is that so?" the duke responded, still eying his political opponent.

Mr. Douglass reluctantly nodded. "Like my father before me, your grace."

"You must come to Brook's with me, then. With strength in numbers, we may be able to enlighten you."

Fanny favored Mr. Douglass with a smile. "Papa would approve."

"Even for Lady Fannia it would be difficult for me to abandon everything I've always believed," Mr. Douglass said.

Annie was surprised he could stand up to Fanny. "As much as I should like to see the number of Whigs swell," Annie said to Mr. Douglass, "I admire your loyalty."

"Loyalty is a most admirable trait, do you not think, your grace?" Fanny asked.

He smiled upon her. "It is indeed. In fact, I am a Whig because of my allegiance to my own father."

Fanny nodded. "Allegiance to one's own family is most admirable."

"It would be exceedingly difficult to admire one who abused his or her sibling, would it not?" Annie asked, factiously eying her twin.

Colour rose into Fanny's cheeks, but the duke did not have the opportunity to observe because Lady Tolworth came into the chamber, and all the gentlemen rose.

She gave the duke the attentions his rank commanded, allowed the other gentlemen to pay her homage, then she took a seat in the middle of the room's largest sofa, a long French piece covered in emerald silk.

Fanny then spoke once more to the duke. "Pray, you grace, did you not know which twin I was straight away today? After all, Annie and I looked vastly different last night."

"I will own," he said, smiling at her, "Had I to guess, I would have guessed correctly."

Fanny nodded. "Just because we're considered identical twins doesn't necessarily mean we must look exactly alike."

"I know mothers of twins never mix up their offspring," Lady Tolworth said, "but even were I not their mother, I would always know one from the other. They are so vastly different."

"Indeed they are," the duke responded, "though I would be incapable of thinking one lovelier than the other. You have two delightfully pretty daughters, Lady Tolworth."

Delightfully pretty? Annie felt as if she actually did possess a rounded bosom.

Each of the other gentlemen agreed.

"Your grace," Mr. Douglass said after all the accolades to their beauty had died down, "when your father was still alive, I had the honor of attending a fete at your home in Richmond."

The duke cocked his head and regarded Mr. Douglass a moment before responding. "We have met before?"

Mr. Douglass shook his head. "No. I'm a few years older than you. I believe you were still at university when I went to Ripley Hall."

"Ah, that explains it. Did you find Ripley Hall to your liking?"

"Very much. How much of my esteem was due to the loveliness of the day or how much to the magnificence of the house would be difficult to calculate."

Nodding, the duke chuckled. "You came from London by river?"

"Indeed."

"Then I perfectly understand your sentiment, Mr. Douglass. There are few things I would rather do on a pretty summer day than float down the River Thames to Ripley. I shall have to invite everyone in this chamber to a picnic there so all of you may judge for yourself."

"I should love it above all things," Fanny exclaimed.

He eyed Annie.

"I should love it, too, but I think your grace may remember what I enjoy above all other things."

A grin creased his sculpted cheeks as he regarded her. "Sitting in the galleries of Parliament listening to a great orator?"

She met his earnest gaze and nodded. She felt such a deep connection with this man.

"To no avail I have beseeched my Annie to care more for the feminine pursuits instead of being the very stamp of her dear father," Lady Tolworth said with a shrug, "but alas, she is what she is."

"She is delightful," he told her mother.

As if overflowing with well-being, she bubbled inside. "I daresay my mother and sister find nothing delightful in politics," Annie said.

"Do you know, Lord Crest," Fanny said to the youthful viscount who sat near their mother, "the duke dislikes balls and assemblies. I cannot credit it for I find them so vastly fun."

"As do I when I have the honor of standing up with one of the lovely Childe twins," Lord Crest replied.

"Though," said Mr. Swinnerton, another caller who would be pleased to secure either sisters' affections, "there are a great many men who do not enjoy assemblies."

Mr. Douglass laughed. "When I was just out of university all I wanted to do was . . ." He stopped himself short.

Annie was relatively certain he was about to admit to an interest in opera dancers and high-stakes play but thought better of it.

". . . spend time with fellows doing things we ought not," Mr. Douglass finished.

Everyone in the chamber laughed.

"Pray, your grace," Fanny asked, lowering her lashes coyly as she spoke, "is that why you avoid assemblies and balls?"

"It's impertinent of you to ask him that," Annie chided.

The duke looked from Annie to Fanny and spoke to the latter in a gentle voice. "Not to worry, my lady. I do spend more time with my long-standing male friends. I prefer to be with those with whom I have much in common."

Then he looked at Annie, no smile on his face this time. This time he looked as serious as a scholar.

Her heartbeat roared in response.

Soon thereafter he took his leave.

* * *

She wasn't like any young woman he'd ever known—not just because she was the only woman he'd known who stamped a red cat's paw on her cheek. He could not purge his thoughts from Lady Annia Childe. She lacked some of the feminine artistry of her lovely sister. In fact, he'd never known a lady who would dare wear the same dress on two consecutive days. Perhaps that's one of the things he found so refreshing about her. She didn't fill her pretty head with useless dribble about fashion and hairdressing. She read not only the greatest thinkers of the age, but she was well informed on issues of government.

Lady Fannia might have a slight edge on appearance, but that mattered not. Both women were possessed of remarkable beauty.

It was Lady Annia, though, whose mind attracted him. Her interests mirrored his own. He found himself wishing to speak to her about the day's great political thinkers. He wanted her opinion on proposed legislation. He enjoyed being in her company—more so than with his male friends. In many respects, he thought of her as a friend. Certainly not one he wished to court.

He hoped his attentions did not send a false message. He had no intentions of becoming suitor to either of the Childe sisters.

Making her acquaintance had resulted in

his most uncharacteristic behavior. Before he'd left Tolworth House the previous night he had surprised himself by announcing his intention to pay a morning call. He never paid morning calls.

After he returned to Axminster House, he went to his library and penned a letter to Lady Tolworth asking her and her daughters to come to Ripley Thursday for a picnic. He would make the Axminster yacht available to them for the purpose.

What manner of change had come over him?

Chapter 3

Thursdays were when Annie visited the lending library on Oxford Street. Fanny did not accompany her today but requested that her sister procure a copy of Voltaire. "I *will* read it," Fanny had said. "I wish to be perceived as intelligent about the great writers."

Now was the time for Annie to get even over her sister's betrayal. "If you wish to appear well-read, you might wish to toss out a little known fact about a famous literary work."

"Such as?"

Annie shrugged. "You could casually mention that most people are unaware that Shakespeare originally thought to name Romeo and Juliet, Henry and Jane, but it was dismissed as being too evocative of Queen Elizabeth's father."

"How amazing!"

Later, as Annie and Eliza were returning to Tolworth House laden with books, Annie chuckled when she pictured Fanny bringing up the topic the next time she was in the presence of the Duke of Axminster. Her heartbeat skipped. When would that be?

At the door to Mama's sitting room, the butler informed Annie that her ladyship had gone out.

Fanny's bedchamber was also unoccupied. Annie walked over to set the copy of Voltaire upon her sister's gilded writing table, and something curious caught her eye. It was a piece of high-quality parchment bearing the crest of the Duke of Axminster. Her pulse thudded. Had she been wrong? Could he prefer Fanny over her? Had Fanny received a communication from him? With a trembling hand, Annie picked up the note. It was not addressed to Fanny but to Mama.

As she read, she felt as if she'd been knocked down by a swiftly moving coach and four. Tears gushed. Her pulse rocketed. Her stomach plummeted. Stunned, it took her a moment to gather her thoughts. The initial disappointment of not seeing Ripley Hall and *him* was pushed aside by the deeper sense of betrayal. Even her mother had betrayed her.

Dazed, she stood there in her sister's bedchamber. The room was a testament to the closeness of the sisters. It was not as nice as Annie's present chamber. It had once been Annie's chamber. Fanny offered her sister the sunlit corner room that had been hers when Annie had been gravely ill with lung fever. Fanny had been distraught.

Now Annie was distraught.

Being morose was against her nature. Of

the two sisters, Annie had always been the pragmatic one. She needed to cast aside her melancholy and form a plan. Her first thoughts were of revenge, but as bitter as she was, Annie had no desire to get mired in ugly fighting.

What, then, did she desire? Most of all, she wanted to be at Ripley Hall right now. She tentatively moved to Fanny's gilded looking glass and peered at herself. She was dressed in the same manner as she would have been were she entertaining callers. Her soft, peach coloured muslin dress cinched her small waist, and its lace-trimmed square neckline almost made her appear womanly.

Her appearance, then, was tolerable. What next? She must find some kind of a vessel to transport her down the River Thames to Ripley. She knew exactly where Ripley Hall was since it was near the Duke of Devonshire's Chiswick, which she had visited several times.

She first asked that the family coach be sent around but was informed that Lady Tolworth and Lady Fannia had left in it. Then she requested a phaeton, and while it was being readied, she fetched Eliza to accompany her. She was not permitted to travel anywhere without a chaperone.

Once they were in the phaeton, progress was slow, owing to the snarl of conveyances between their house in Mayfair and the river.

More than once her horse came to a complete stop. "We may have been better off walking," she hissed.

"'Tis just a minor delay. Don't fret. We'll be there in a thrice."

Her hopes of finding a fine sailing vessel were dashed when she reached the docking area. Only one craft was there. It was a small yawl piled with a mountain of potatoes. Its only seat was occupied by the gray-haired man piloting the vessel.

She handed over the reins of her horse to the stable lad who'd ridden on the phaeton's tiger's mount. "Wait to see if we're successful in boarding. If we are, you may return."

She then approached the man in the yawl. "Sir. Are you by chance going to pass through Richmond?"

"Aye." One of his front teeth was missing.

She reached into her reticule and retrieved a crown. "I'd be so grateful if you'd allow my maid and me to ride with you for the short trip to Richmond." She knew they would have to sit upon the dirty potatoes. Perhaps he had a cloth upon which they could sit.

He eyed the coin, then her. "You'd pay me a crown?"

"Indeed."

His craggy face brightened. "Ye're welcome to get in, but I ain't got nothing for ye to sit on but the potatoes I'm taking up to Oxford."

"We'll manage." She hurried to the slip,

and he assisted first her, then Eliza.

* * *

When he saw Lady Tolworth approach the terrace with just one daughter, Alex frowned. Even from this distance, he was certain this was the wrong twin. Everything in her confident, coquettish demeanor told him this sister was Lady Fannia. Where was Annie? In his mind, he was beginning to think of the smart twin by the name her family used.

They were joined by the same gentlemen who'd sat in the Tolworth drawing room two days earlier, and all of them were smiling warmly at the Childe women. Regarding the females through narrowed eyes, he said, "I perceive you've come without Lady Annia?"

Lady Fannia giggled. "How flattering, your grace, that in so short a time you've come to know one of us from the other. No other men are as perceptive as you." She dipped into a curtsy then offered him her outstretched hand to kiss.

He kissed the air above it whilst locking gazes with the mother. She too curtsied. After the exchanges of greetings with all his guests, he went back to Lady Tolworth. "I do hope Lady Annia has not taken ill."

"Thank you for your interest, your grace. My other daughter enjoys robust health." She lifted her head heavenward. "Thanks to the good Lord. Truth to tell, I thought she would be accompanying us today, but she made her excuses to Fanny. My Annie loves her books. Thursday is the day she goes to both the lending library and to the booksellers."

It stung that she preferred books to him. The day he had so enthusiastically looked forward to now seemed like the worst sort of drudgery. His only purpose in inviting Tuesday's group to his house today was to have the opportunity to be with Annie. For some unexplainable reason, he wanted to show her this property that meant so much to him. He'd wondered if she would admire it as he did.

Out of the blue, he wondered if she had given her heart to another man. Was that why she had not come? The idea of losing his new-found friend to matrimony bothered him.

Despite the sun and mild temperatures which would otherwise have made this a very fine day, nothing could dispel his gloom. He must try to play the consummate host even if his heart was no longer invested in the endeavor. He led the group from the terrace which ran the entire width of Ripley Hall down to a meadow near the river. There his servants had set up a two tables, dressed them with ironed cloths, and began to unpack hampers. Another set about removing corks from the wine bottles.

Lady Fannia wasted no time in sidling up to him. "Where will you sit, your grace, for I plan to sit near so you can enlighten me on the history of this beautiful place."

His demeanor was cool when he responded. "I prefer that you sit near Mr. Douglass. A man who goes to such lengths to write sonnets in praise of your beauty, my lady, must reap some reward."

"But . . ."

Before she could respond, he turned to her mother. "You, my lady, must sit near me."

Mr. Douglass, the viscount, and Mr. Swinnerton counted themselves fortunate to be seated near the lovely Lady Fannia.

As Alex sat down with Lady Tolworth, she launched into a catalogue of Lady Fannia's attributes.

When she paused, he asked, "And what is your husband doing today?" It was obvious to him that Annie was the embodiment of her father. Only in a pretty way.

He barely listened to her ladyship's response for his thoughts were on the missing daughter.

Sudden and distant cries prevented them from taking the first bite. It sounded like a woman in distress. Or possibly two.

He leapt up. "Someone's drowning!" He started running toward the Thames, the others following.

Before they reached his small dock, he could see that a yawl had pulled up there, and a gray-haired man appeared to be attempting to rescue two bedraggled women, but one was too far away from him.

As Alex came closer, he could have sworn the woman farthest away was Annie. His chest exploded, his step quickened. He raced to the water's edge and dove in.

He came to the water's surface just where Annie was struggling to keep her wet head above water. The river was deep here, so deep his feet couldn't touch the bottom. He hauled her into his arms and treaded water toward the shore, where a family of mallards was scurrying to get away.

Douglass, who was standing at the river bank, reached for Annie and helped to pull her drenched body from the water. Both of them fell, and one stray mallard promptly landed on her lap.

The gray-haired man and another lady were already standing there, dripping wet.

Damn, but that water was cold! With Lord Crest assisting him, Alex climbed onto the quay and went straight to Annie. He lifted her in his arms. One of Alex's footmen relieved her of the duck and faced his master, the duck's bottom aimed at the Duke of Axminster's face. For the second time in a week, Alex found himself in the undignified position of facing a creature's rear end. "Pitch it back into the water," Alex snapped.

He began to stride back to his house. He had to get her warm. There was no telling how long she had been in that water.

"What the devil?" he finally asked her.

"My maid fell in and I foolishly thought to save her."

"But you cannot swim."

She nodded gravely. "Terribly stupid of me."

"I didn't know Lady Annia could be stupid." He looked down at her affectionately and saw that her cheek featured a muddy print of a duck's webbed foot. What the devil? First, a red cat's paw, and now this.

The disarray of her hair that first night would now look lovely by comparison to today's. Yet as he looked at the soggy mass, he could see that beneath her normally powdered tresses her hair was a lovely shade of blonde—somewhere between flax and white. It made her look all the more delicate.

He hugged her to him. "I'm glad you've come." Even if she did display a muddy duck foot upon her lovely face.

* * *

Even the glow from being held in *his* arms, from hearing his *I'm glad you've come* could not dispel her misery. The water had been very cold, and even now she was chilled from her trembling lips to the tips of her icy toes. She could not stop shaking. Even her teeth rattled.

On top of her physical misery, she was mortified over her humiliating entrance. And how pitiable she must look! She was also incredibly remorseful that she had caused the poor duke to dive into those murky waters. He must be as miserable as she, but he continued to stride up the slope without even getting winded—or without his teeth chattering.

This was far worse than the day she lost her drawers.

The others were gathering around. That's when Mama recognized her. She screamed. It was more of a wail, actually. "My Annie! Dear merciful Savior! She's drowned!" She covered hers eyes. "I cannot look. Fanny! Has your sister drowned?"

Fanny's voice choked when she answered. "It's all my fault! I've killed her." She began to sob. "The one I love best."

In spite of her twin's incredible selfishness, deep down she loved Annie. *Best.* Annie was too touched to display anger. "I. Am. Not. Dead," she managed between staccato clashes of upper teeth against lower.

By now a drenched Eliza came up beside her and the duke, matching the duke's long stride. "I'm ever so sorry, milady." Her teeth, too, were clattering. "For tumbling into the water. And for not knowing how to swim."

"I'm just happy neither of us drowned," Annie said.

"I'm thankful our driver knew how to swim so he could rescue me," Eliza said.

Lady Tolworth hurried to come abreast of

them. "What do you man *our driver*? What means of transport brought you here?"

"We came in the potato boat, milady."

Lady Tolworth gasped and clutched at her chest. "Do not tell me my daughter was conveyed here on a potato boat!"

Now Annie's humiliation was complete. She'd thought no one would see her arrival, no one would see the conveyance in which she had come to Ripley Hall.

"Quick! My vinaigrette!" Lady Tolworth demanded. "I'm certain I am going to faint."

Whilst Lady Tolworth was sighing heavily and ranting about the potato boat, Fanny claimed the vinaigrette, opened it and passed the *sal volatile* in it beneath her mother's nose several times.

Annie wished she could faint—or die of mortification to extricate herself from her misery.

Several of the Axminster footmen had come to assist. The duke called to them. "Go into the house and see that there's a fire in each fireplace."

She couldn't reach a fireplace too soon.

When he reached the top of the slope and level land, the cream-coloured brick of Ripley came into view. It was not an excessively large house, but it was sheer perfection. Perfectly symmetrical, it was in the Palladian style. A few steps led up to a long, classically balustraded terrace that fronted the structure.

She was anxious to enter and especially anxious to feel the fires. Once they entered the dinner room directly off the terrace, he turned to Lady Tolworth. "You will have to see that your daughter gets out of these wet clothes." They entered a corridor that led to the home's main staircase, and he began to mount the steps, with her mother, sister, and maid directly behind.

She found herself staring at the Axminster family portraits that lined the stairwell. Those black eyes, she decided, were a dominant family trait. Few of the long-dead stodgy looking men were in possession of blue or green eyes.

At the top of the stairwell was a portrait of a beautiful woman. From her clothing, Annie judged the painting to have been painted no more than thirty years ago. The dark-haired woman effected a faint smile. *His smile.* "Your mother?"

"Yes."

"She's lovely."

"She still is some thirty years later. Hopefully, she'll have clothing that you and your maid can wear." His gaze dropped to her slender waist. "It may be a little large, but at least it will be dry."

"I shall be most grateful." The chattering of her teeth had finally abated.

He brought her to a sumptuous

bedchamber of white, turquoise, and much gilt. The turquoise draperies were all open, and the room was flooded with sunlight. Best of all, a fire roared in the grate.

"This is my mother's bedchamber, but she's not at Ripley at present." He set her down on the silken bed. "I'll have dry clothes sent right around."

Eliza, whose clothing was not only more modest than her mistress's but also less complicated, was capable of removing her own.

After the door shut behind him, Mama rushed to Annie and began to assist in removing the sodden clothing, continuing to rant about the potato boat. To Fanny, she said, "Under no circumstances are you ever to tell anyone about Annie's humiliation. She paused to dramatically cover her eyes. "I am mortified the Duke of Axminster had to witness your embarrassing entrance. Why could you not have stayed home? It's not as if you are romantically interested in the duke."

"But there you're wrong," Annie whispered. "I wanted to come here more than anything."

Annie moved to stand in front of the blazing fire, still shivering. "Why, Mama, did you not tell me about the picnic? It was wrong to exclude me."

"Oh, my dearest, that was never my intention. I gave the invitation to Fanny, and it never occurred to me she would not share it with you." Lady Tolworth draped Annie's pretty muslin dress over a chair in front of the fire. Unfortunately the back of it was dirty—from the potatoes. *Why didn't I stay home?*

Lady Tolworth addressed her other daughter. "I shall be most vexed with you, Fanny, for lying to me. Have I not always told you how wicked it is to lie?"

Fanny looked contrite. "I didn't actually lie. It's true I never showed Annie the invitation. Then today I merely told you that Annie had chosen to go to the lending library and the book shop."

Annie's mouth dropped open. "Which was most certainly a lie!"

"Not actually."

"You are a devious cheat."

The sisters glared at one another.

"I'm sorry," Fanny said solemnly. "It was wrong of me. I wanted the duke to myself."

"Dearest?" Lady Tolworth stared at Annie. "Why do you have a duck foot on your face?"

Annie raced to the looking glass. Had she looked like that in front of the Duke of Axminster? *I must be cursed.*

There was a knock at the door. Lady Tolworth opened the door a sliver, then relieved a maid of the dresses piled high in her arms.

Annie chose a lovely ivory muslin trimmed in thick white lace. Unfortunately it was two inches too short for her, and the waist several inches too wide. After she dressed and stepped in front of the looking glass, her heart fell. She looked like a parlor maid dressing up in her mistress's clothing. She felt like weeping. "I should never have come."

"I do wish you hadn't—not just because of the humiliation from the potato boat." Lady Tolworth sighed and blinked back tears. "I thought you'd drowned. I've never had such a fright."

By now Eliza had put on a frothy green dress and came to Annie. "Don't fret about yer hair. I'll have it pretty as a portrait." She came and began to remove all the pins. "Let it down then turn upside down as close to the fire as you can stand. It will dry quickly that way."

The duke sent around a note. It was addressed to Lady Tolworth, who read it aloud.

My Dear Lady Tolworth,

Under the present circumstances, I think it advisable that you and your daughters stay the night at Ripley. I shouldn't like to expose Lady Annia to a further chill after her ordeal. She was submerged for quite some time in that frigid water. Since your daughter's size in no way corresponds to that of my mother—who is at present at our country seat—I have taken the liberty of sending round to Tolworth House for fresh dresses for the ladies in your family. I also took the liberty of charging your own personal maid with the task of gathering clothing for your twins. I pray my plans are agreeable to you.

Also, tonight's dinner gathering will be comprised of those who were here this afternoon. All of the gentlemen have agreed to stay.

--Axminster

Now that Annie was dry and relatively thawed, she allowed herself to reflect on the duke's words. *I'm glad you've come.* How touched she'd been. And to think, he'd dived into the filthy water to save her! So gallant a man would likely have dived into the water to save anyone in distress, nevertheless, she believed that just as he was her special someone, she was special to him too.

But could he merely be thinking fondly of her as he would a close friend? Could he possibly ever desire her in a certain way?

It was up to her to see that he did. But how?

$\mathcal{C}$hapter 4

After Alex shed his own wet clothing and redressed, he came to stand in front of the fire in his dressing room. He couldn't purge from his mind the vision of Lady Annia flailing about in that water, begging for someone to help her. For a few seconds, he had feared she would drown. He'd been seized with fear before he dove into the water.

It was impossible to explain the myriad emotions that overcame him when he knew she was unhurt. He was so thankful he'd been outdoors and heard her cries. The gray-haired man would never have been able to reach her—not when he had his hands full with her maid. It sickened Alex to think of Lady Annia dead.

In a short time she had become very special to him—not that he intended to offer marriage. He had no desire to be married. Besides, theirs was not that sort of relationship.

His thoughts then moved to her manner of conveyance. What the devil was the daughter of an earl doing on a potato boat? The only explanation was that she was determined to get to Ripley. He was relieved. She must enjoy his company as much as he enjoyed hers.

Then it struck him why Lady Annia had not come with her mother and sister. The sister was blatant about her desire to snare him. Had she purposely left without her twin? Perhaps not told her the correct time?

He vowed that at dinner he would see to it that Lady Fannia understood he had no interest in her. All his interest—which was *not* romantic—was in Lady Annia.

Annie also was *not* the type of woman one wanted to seduce. The thought of another man attempting seduction on her angered him. He knew now he shouldn't have invited Viscount Crest to Ripley. The man was far too interested in her. Alex had watched him as he watched Lady Annia. Alex's hands fisted.

It was still several hours before dinner. He had pushed back the dining time in order to ensure the ladies' dresses arrived. He'd also sent another note to ask that Lord Tolworth join them. He drew a deep breath. He would go to the billiards room and attempt to play the role of congenial host. Except to Lord Crest, he thought, frowning.

* * *

One could learn much about flirting by watching her twin, but Annie could never act as she did. For one thing, none of Fanny's flirting had succeeded in garnering the duke's favor. During the long afternoon, Annie had thought about what she could do to capture the duke's affections. The battle was half won since she knew he favored her. But how could she win his heart? He'd guarded it for many years. She'd looked him up in Burke's Peerage and learned that he was thirty. Time to settle down.

She had no doubts they were made for one another. How compatible they would be! How gratifying it would be to spend every day with the person who was one's best friend. If only he weren't a lofty duke.

A pity there was no rival to make him jealous. She believed a rival could make him see her as something other than a friend.

The first step to attracting was to insure she could to look her best. After her hair dried, Eliza arranged it smartly. They found a powder room and powdered it lightly. She hoped the duke didn't see her racing through the corridor in his mother's ill-fitting dress. She moved quickly in the hopes of avoiding him. She had embarrassed herself enough for one day.

It was long after their normal dinner hour when the footman returned with evening dresses for the Childe ladies. She had feared that without Eliza there to guide her, Mama's maid would not choose well, but Annie was pleased with the scarlet velvet.

It should remind his grace that she was a woman.

* * *

Alex had dressed for dinner early and come down in case any of his guests were also early. He'd explained to the other three gentlemen that since they were in the country and since a near-catastrophic incident had occurred that day, their inability to dress in dinner clothing would be excused.

He came to the marble entry hall just as his footmen swept in with armloads of fine dresses, and right behind them, Lord Tolworth came.

Alex was at first taken aback when the earl did not smile at him.

"Where's my Annie? I was told she'd drowned." Lord Tolworth's voice broke.

"Thank God," Alex said, "I was able to reach her in time. I expect a full recovery."

Lord Tolworth buried his head in hands for a few seconds, then looked up at Alex. "I am deeply in your debt. What in the bloody hell happened?"

"All I know is that she jumped in the river to save her maid."

"But she can't swim!"

Alex nodded. "Your highly intelligent daughter has acknowledged her error."

"That does sound like my Annie."

Did Lord Tolworth ever refer to Lady Fannia as *my Fanny*? Alex could not remember him doing so.

At dinner nearly an hour later, Alex sat at

the head of the table where he had so carefully arranged the seating. He'd asked Lady Tolworth, as the highest ranking woman, to be his hostess and preside over the foot of the table. To make his lack of intentions clear, he'd seated her daughter Lady Fannia beside her. He had the highest ranking man, Lord Tolworth, on one side of him, and Lady Annia on his other side. That scoundrel Lord Crest was seated to Lady Tolworth's other side. Let him press his attentions on the other twin!

Alex started off by lifting his claret glass. "A toast of thanks that Lady Annia is still with us." Their glasses clinked together. Lord Tolworth could not remove his eyes from Lady Annia. "You gave your mother and me a terrible fright."

"*I* have never had such a fright!" Annie exclaimed. Her gaze then softened and she peered at Alex. "If you'd not been outdoors and heard my cries, I daresay I'd be at the bottom of the Thames right now."

Her mother shrieked, her father winced.

"It was a terrifying situation, to be sure," Alex said.

"I am deeply grateful to you and deeply apologetic that you had to plunge into the cold, murky water to save me."

"Don't give it a second thought. I rather fancy being the rescuer of maidens in distress."

The three of them laughed.

Mr. Swinnerton, who sat at Lady Annia's right, said, "I shall be most vexed that the duke arrived at the river first, my lady, because I would have given my own life to save yours."

She turned to Swinnerton, all smiles and crinkly eyes. "You always say the sweetest things. How gallant you are!"

As far as Alex was concerned, there was nothing gallant in *saying* one would lay down his life. Why had he not previously noticed how annoying that Swinnerton was? A pity Alex had invited him--him and that cocksure Lord Crest.

Alex addressed her. "So, have you decided on Warren Hastings' guilt?"

"Seeing as how the gentleman's offenses occurred in India, I am not in a position to judge him, nor would I wish to judge anyone without knowing all the facts."

His feelings exactly. "And you, your lordship?" he asked her father.

Lord Tolworth directed a shimmering gaze on his daughter. "I taught my Annie well. I couldn't agree more with her opinions. Though, as a Whig, I am inclined to align myself with those who will be attempting to prosecute him."

Alex shrugged. "There is that. I know I would hate to go up against Burke."

"It will be magnificent to watch the

proceedings in the House of Lords," Annie said. "I understand Fanny Burney's to be in the galleries."

"I daresay people will be fighting to claim a seat there," Alex acknowledged.

"In Mr. Hastings' behalf, I will mention that it's obvious he never amassed in India the kind of vast wealth that Clive did," she said. "Does that not point to his innocence on corruption charges?"

"An astute observation, to be sure, my lady," Alex said. "That's the kind of evidence that Hastings' counsel needs to introduce."

"Annie's already beseeched me to procure a seat for her in the gallery," Lord Tolworth said.

Alex regarded her with an amused gaze.

"It would be my honor, my lady," Mr. Swinnerton said, "to escort you there."

Alex fumed. Why couldn't that demmed Swinnerton be addressing his attentions to the other twin?

Annie turned to Swinnerton. "How kind of you to ask. I should love it."

"Did you see the subscription in the paper for Lord Petersham?" Lord Tolworth asked no one in particular.

Annie replied. "I did. Allow me to say I feel no remorse for a man who's foolishly lost his fortune at the gaming tables. I wouldn't lift a finger to help such a man."

"While you and I normally see eye to eye,"

her father said to her, "I can't agree with your harsh sentiments. The man was only doing what all his contemporaries are doing."

"I think it's a weak man who falls prey to high-stakes gaming and loses all that his illustrious family has built over centuries. How is that man seeing to the well-being of his own family?"

Alex was inclined to agree with her.

Lord Tolworth shrugged. "Well, of course, when that man has a family . . ."

"Which Lord Petersham has," she added.

"Then, my dear daughter, you are right."

Was this young woman always right? He could not remove his eyes from the loveliness of her flawless face. The candlelight flickered in her pale eyes. How lovely she was. Quite naturally, his eye traveled from that remarkable face down her graceful neck to her ivory chest where the promise of a woman's breasts dipped beneath the red velvet.

His breath grew short. He experienced an overwhelming urge to remove that velvet gown and luxuriate in the feel of her, to settle his lips on hers, to . . .

He could not allow his thoughts to go there. This young woman was a friend. Only a friend. And she was the daughter of a great friend. One did not debauch such maidens.

"Your grace?"

His gaze met Lady Fannia's on the opposite

end of the table.

"We have been discussing the greatest writers. Do you agree that Shakespeare has no equal?"

"I do."

"I adore his works," Lady Fannia said. "Did you know that *Romeo and Juliet* was originally to be titled Harry and Jane?"

It sounded preposterously erroneous to him.

Her father glared down the table at his other daughter. "You mustn't propagate such drivel, girl! Everyone knows Shakespeare used Italian names for his plays set in that country. Though how a humble man from Stratford-upon-Avon came to be so brilliant is a mystery to me."

Alex did not want to overtly stare at the now-humiliated twin, but he could not help but to notice how she had finally—for the first time since he'd known her—clammed up. It was remarkable how two ladies with identical appearances could be so dissimilar in intelligence."So," Lord Tolworth said to the smart twin, "why were you bringing your maid today when you were traveling with your mother and sister?"

"I was not traveling with my mother and sister," she said solemnly, her eyelids downcast. "They forgot to tell me of his grace's invitation."

Lord Tolworth shot an angry glare down

the table to his other twin daughter.

"I cannot tell you how gratified I am, my lady," Alex said, trying to smooth over the sudden awkwardness, "that you found out about my planned picnic and contrived your own means of transport. This gathering would have been sadly flat without you."

Her face coloured.

Was she embarrassed over the potato boat?

"I was vastly interested in seeing Ripley Hall. It is widely praised," she said.

His eyes danced. "Permit me to take you on a private tour of it after dinner."

* * *

After the men finished their port and joined the ladies in the drawing room, the duke said, "Since Lady Annia went to such great lengths today to see Ripley, I shall give her an exclusive tour now." He eyed Lady Fannia, who was just about to open her mouth. "The rest of you, if you so desire, can have my housekeeper show you around the old pile in the morning."

He moved to Annie and offered his arm. Fanny was glaring at her. Annie felt like the wallflower who'd just been tapped to stand up with the prince. Only this was a thousand times better. For as much as she loved her sister, Annie confessed to gloating over Fanny's disappointment.

The duke started his tour at the front door. "Unlike most houses, where the entrance faces the carriage drive, this opens to the river," he said.

Even though they had entered the house earlier in the day through the dinner room, she had caught a glimpse of the entry hall while he carried her in his arms, but she had not seen much. She'd been too busy burying her face into his shoulders so no one could see how hideous she looked with those great masses of wet hair.

Now her gaze swung from the door along the checkered marble entry which soared up to a domed roof. The wide staircase was every bit as opulent as the hallway.

From the hall, several rooms gave off. The first was a pale green morning room, sparsely furnished but with rich silken draperies embellished with gold cording and tassels.

"Here's the family's parlor," he said when they entered the second chamber. "We take breakfast here when Mama and my sisters are in residence." He sighed. "My brother, too, before he was posted to Paris as ambassador."

"It sounds as if you miss him."

"I do."

"It's a lovely room, and so intimate." Her gaze circled the chamber. A round table, large enough for four or five people, was placed near the tall casement. "East facing. You must get the morning light here. In the daylight I expect you've a lovely vista of green lawns and trees."

"Yes, we do. It's a welcome respite from London's nasty air."

She sighed. "How fortunate you are to have such a haven so close to the capital."

"Do not think me unappreciative."

The next chamber was the library. "This is my domain," he said. It looked like him. So solid with the dark woods and crimson upholstery. A fire blazed in the hearth. Like the other rooms at Ripley, it was not overly large. It was even more intimate than the family's morning room.

He walked to the fireplace and stood before it. She could not remove her gaze from him. No man had ever been as handsome, as appealing. It wasn't just his height. It certainly wasn't because he was a duke. It was just *him*. Everything about this dark paragon ignited something in her. Something alien, something she had never before experienced.

His brows lowered. "Why do you stare? Is something wrong?"

She shook her head. "No, nothing. I was just . . . thinking how well this chamber suits you." She had gone and embarrassed herself again. To divert his attention, she strolled to the books and began reading titles.

"Did you select the books, or were these inherited?"

"About half and half." He moved to her and

pointed to the very shelf she was peering at. "These are mine."

She had scanned the titles on two long shelves. "I see no poetry here. How singular."

"I should be ashamed to admit it, but I'm not a lover of poems."

A little laugh broke from her. "It's the same with me."

"Has it struck you that we a very much alike, Annie?"

Her heartbeat pounded. He had called her by her Christian name! No man other than her father had ever addressed her by that name. She dare not allow herself to peer into his eyes for he would know what a hopeless fool she was to adore him.

Her gaze latched onto Gibbon's Roman history, and she pulled it out. "I'm eagerly looking forward to the release of the second volume. Are you, your grace?" She opened the book and flipped through the pages. She hoped he did not notice her hands were trembling—because he had called her *Annie*. And because he was so close. Still she refrained from looking up at him. She was not certain she wouldn't make a cake of herself by launching herself into his arms. He was so near she could smell his sandalwood scent.

He braced himself with one arm on the bookcase as he leaned even closer and spoke in a husky voice. "I am." His head began to lower. "But I'm more eagerly looking forward to this." His lips touched hers softly.

She drew in her breath but could not have pulled away had the roof collapsed around them. The kiss intensified. She put her arms around him, sighing as she continued the intoxicating kiss.

He drew her into his arms and held her tightly, as if he were afraid she would flee.

Finally he pulled away and stiffened. "Forgive me." Then he turned and left the chamber.

Chapter 5

Even if it meant being a shameful host, he was far too rattled to return to the drawing room. He stormed out the front door and began to pace the lawns, careful to keep out of view from the windows. What the devil had come over him? Alex had never in his life acted so rashly. Always before he'd been the one to consider every decision from every angle—particularly on how it would impact others. That came from being the firstborn, the one responsible for his younger siblings.

But not tonight. Ever since he'd met Lady Annia Childe, he'd been surprising himself with uncharacteristic behavior. That first night he'd met her, right out of the blue, he had announced his intention of paying a morning call at Tolworth House. He *never* paid morning calls! He couldn't even remember contemplating calling on Lady Annia, but it just blurted out of his mouth as if he'd been possessed by someone else.

That same alien force must have been responsible for the picnic. He'd never hosted a picnic. Until he met Annie.

And the kiss, that scorching kiss! A man of

honor simply did not go about stealing kisses from well-born maidens, especially from a well-born maiden whose father was exceedingly well respected. Such a maiden was sure to take it in her head the kiss meant more than it did. And that was the last thing he wanted.

Besides marriage. He'd been well satisfied with his bachelor life.

His heartbeat hitched. He'd also been well satisfied with Annie's kiss. The very memory of it flowed to his aching groin. He'd been so pleased when her arms had come around him that he'd actually groaned his pleasure.

Even as he stood there in the moonlight, his gaze traveling down to the shimmering Thames, he wanted more of Annie's kisses. But he did not want to offer her false hope. He had no intentions of marrying. And Annie wasn't one to be misused.

She was far too precious. He realized now she was somewhat more than a friend. He had many friends, many good friends, but he'd never wanted to kiss any of them.

Good Lord, what had he done? He could not blame his contrariness on an alien force. He and he alone was responsible for all these uncharacteristic actions. An incalculable change had come over him since making the acquaintance of one very lovely, amusing young woman who just happened to kiss exceedingly well.

* * *

She continued to stand in the library, dazed by the effect his magical kiss had on her. Her entire body quivered. During those moments of The Kiss, an indefinable sense of well-being had come over her. And when his arms came around her, she could have swooned from pure joy. Nothing in her life had ever felt so good, so right. In his arms was where she was meant to be.

Now she knew she had truly fallen in love with Alex Halsey, the Duke of Axminster. *Alex.*

But he obviously did not feel the same.

When he fled, she'd felt more bereft than a deposed queen. Had the inadequacy of her kiss repelled him? She had no experience in such matters. She'd never before been kissed. And kissed in return. He must have been dissatisfied with her lack of kissing skill. How she wanted to tell him she would learn! Oh, how she would enjoy practicing with him— her tall, dark lover.

The very fact that he'd crossed the library to initiate the kiss must confirm that he *was* attracted to her. Didn't the fiery look in his black eyes or the huskiness of his voice as he lowered his head to touch her lips indicate a desired intimacy? She'd felt womanly and desirable for the first time in her life.

For those few moments of the kiss she'd even felt cherished.

Then he'd left abruptly with no explanation. Except his *Forgive me.* Could it be it wasn't the inadequacy of her kisses that drove him away? Could it be he was ashamed of his own impetuousness?

She sighed. Knowing him as she did, she thought the last explanation correct, but that only made her feel more dejected. A man in love would not regret kissing his future wife. Only an honorable man who had no honorable intentions would feel such remorse. Alex was an honorable man.

Who had no honorable intentions toward her.

Annie had never been one to give up, and she wasn't about to give up now. The stakes were too high. Alex would be her perfect mate, and she knew he could search the kingdom and never find another who was more compatible.

Her obstacle was his obvious opposition to marriage. Her ally was his affection for her. In spite of his abandonment tonight, she knew he cared deeply for her. He had insured that she sat by him at dinner. He had excluded everyone in order to take her on a private tour of Ripley. And he had not been able to suppress his desire to kiss her. Her heartbeat fluttered at the memory.

He needed a push in order to realize his feelings. He needed to think he was about to lose her.

* * *

When she was walking to her bedchamber, she heard muffled cries outside Fanny's chamber. Oh, dear. Fanny must be upset because the duke showed favoritism to her. She drew in a breath and knocked. "Fanny, it's me, Annie."

Handkerchief in hand, Fanny came and swept open the door.

Annie hugged her. "Pray, dearest, what is wrong?" She hated asking. She hated being the source of her sister's misery, but she would begrudgingly become estranged from Fanny rather than give up Alex. It didn't bear contemplation. Part of her would die if she were lost to Fanny.

"Papa has just left my chamber." Sniff. "He told me how wicked I was to exclude you from today's picnic." Fanny began to sob—gut-wrenching sobs that racked her body as she flung herself on her bed.

Though Papa was right to chastise her, Annie hated to watch her sister in such misery. She went to the bed and spoke soft, soothing words as she patted her. "What's past is past, dearest. Nothing harmed."

With one final heaving sob, Fanny sat up and took the fresh handkerchief Annie offered. "I almost killed you."

"What are you talking about?" Annie asked.

"If you had drowned, it would have been my fault."

That was partially true. "Thankfully, the duke rescued me from such a fate."

Now Fanny leaned over and encircled Annie with both arms and held her tightly. "I'm so sorry. I would have died if you did. I love you more than I love anyone."

Tears welled in Annie's eyes.

"And," Fanny continued, "I realize now all my wickedness was in vain. The duke is in love with you, and I wish you every happiness with him."

"Thank you. I do believe he may love me, but he doesn't know it yet."

"Then you must see that he discovers it. You two are perfect for one another."

"I wish I knew how to go about that."

"Leave it to me."

* * *

When the sisters entered the dining room the following morning, Papa was sitting there talking to Mr. Douglass. Empty plates in front of them indicated they had already eaten. The twins joined Mr. Swinnerton at the sideboard where the three of them helped themselves to the breakfast offerings.

As Annie was slathering freshly-churned butter onto her toast, Fanny addressed Mr. Swinnerton. "Since my poor sister was unable to see the gardens of Ripley yesterday afternoon, I was hoping you could show them to her after breakfast. I would myself, but Mr. Douglass has offered to take me to the chapel."

Mr. Swinnerton smiled upon Annie. "I would be honored to take you about the gardens—after you eat, of course."

"Thank you. I shall look forward to it." She would much rather stroll through the rich green lawns on Alex's arm.

A cup of tea in one hand, and a small plate in the other, Annie came to sit next to her father.

Lord Tolworth smiled upon her. "Mr. Douglass was just telling me that power should be vested only in the ruling class, and that our class will see to it that citizens will be taken care of."

She raised her brows, eyeing Mr. Douglass, who was the grandson of a duke. "Not to disparage *you*, but your thinking belongs in the Dark Ages. We are in the age of Enlightenment."

"It's glad I am that women are not permitted to serve in Parliament," Mr. Douglass said with smile.

From the corner of her eye, Annie saw Alex enter the chamber. Her heartbeat stampeded. Even her breath grew short with the memory of their intimacy the previous night. She went mute.

All the guests greeted their host as he poured a cup of tea. "Your grace must come sit by us," Lord Tolworth said. "My daughter has been chastising poor Douglass over his

Tory beliefs. The presence of our host might have the effect of making Annie behave more civilly."

Alex chuckled as his gaze flicked from Annie to her father. "While your daughter is possessed of strong beliefs, I choose not to rein her in since her opinions align with mine." He came to sit next to Mr. Douglass, opposite of Annie.

"You're not eating, your grace?" she asked.

"I ate much earlier."

Lord Tolworth peered at his host. "So you had difficulty sleeping?"

Alex laughed to himself. "You know me too well, my lord."

Annie wondered if he lost sleep for the same reason that robbed her of sleep the previous night—The Kiss as well as his strange reaction to it.

Alex turned to Mr. Douglass, smiling broadly. "I do hope Lord Tolworth's opinionated daughter isn't being uncivil to a guest in my house." Then with a wink, he eyed Annie.

"Oh, no, your grace," Mr. Douglass sputtered. "Lady Annia and I are used to verbal sparring."

"We have to put up with Mr. Douglass nearly every day," Annie said facetiously, rolling her eyes even as she smiled.

"I, for one, enjoy Mr. Douglass's visits," said Fanny, who had sat at the other side of the

Scotsman.

The tender look Mr. Douglass gave Fanny could have melted the butter on the sideboard.

"You do believe the franchise should be extended, do you not, your grace?" Annie asked.

His black eyes met hers. "I may be shooting myself in the foot, but I most certainly do. The power is vested in too few."

"His grace should know," her father said. "He controls eight and thirty seats in Parliament—thankfully seats he's insured are occupied by Whigs."

"Such changes are not likely to come in our lifetime," Annie said, "but it's gratifying to know men like you and my father will work toward such reforms."

Lord Crest entered the chamber, and after he piled his plate very high, came to sit to the other side of Annie. His brows lowered as he squinted at her. "Lady Annia, is it not?"

She nodded. "Bravo, Lord Crest. Few gentlemen have ever been able to tell one of us from the other." She eyed Mr. Douglass. "I believe Mr. Douglass is the only one."

"I have," the duke said, an adversarial tone in his voice.

"I . . . wasn't sure if you were sure," she said.

His voice softened. "I would know you anywhere, my lady."

His comment sent her pulse racing again. Coming from his lips, she fancied it was a romantic statement.

"I do hope, Lady Annia, that you have suffered no ill effects from your plunge into the Thames yesterday," Lord Crest said.

"No ill effects," she said. Somehow, dear Eliza had contrived to clean the potato dirt and muddy duck prints from yesterday's dress, so a modicum of Annie's confidence had been restored as she wore the feminine dress.

"In fact," Mr. Swinnerton said, "Lady Annia has done me the honor of permitting me to take her through the duke's gardens." He eyed her. "Are your finished eating, my lady?"

She noted his plate was clean, even though he'd had twice as much food as she'd taken. She would much rather spend the morning sitting around this table talking politics with her father and Alex, but she knew she must go along with Fanny's scheme.

Hopefully, it would be successful in igniting Alex's passions—especially passion for her.

"Certainly, my lord," she said, smiling up at the man as if she worshipped him, leaving her chair.

Alex glared at Mr. Swinnerton. "I'd suggest you not take long. If it's agreeable to Lord and Lady Tolworth, the yacht will be ready to take all of you back at one o'clock."

* * *

Once again Annie was responsible for his uncharacteristic behavior. Because of her he was being an abominable host. Once she'd left the eating room, he did too. He wanted to watch her as she explored *his* grounds with that arrogant Swinnerton. Stewing in ill humor, Alex would not have been good company had he stayed in the dinner room. He had looked forward to showing her Ripley. Of all his properties, Ripley was his favorite. He had envisioned strolling through the verdant grounds with her on his arm.

Of course he had made a mess of showing her the house last night. Why had he gone and kissed her like that? It was far from being a platonic kiss. Hell, it was far from being a chaste kiss! He had wanted to ravish her.

The very memory of it made something within him ache. It was like a huge, gaping void where his heart should be.

He wondered if Swinnerton would try to kiss her. Suddenly, the prospect of hurling a fist into the smug Swinnerton's face held great appeal. Better yet, shove him into the Thames and hope he could not swim.

He started to go to the library because it had several windows from which he could see his grounds, but he couldn't go there. Not now, not when the memory of their kiss was so fresh. And so debilitating.

Instead, he went upstairs to his own chambers, and from there he watched Annie stroll along the garden paths on Swinnerton's arm, smiling up at him and laughing. What the devil could the two of them find to discuss? To Alex's knowledge, Swinnerton did not even try to serve in Parliament. Did the man have no sense of public service? Was he completely given to the pursuit of pleasure? He likely went about debauching innocent maidens. He'd better not try to take liberties with Annie! Alex determined he would not leave his post at this window. It was imperative that he watch Annie. She needed to be protected from libertines like Swinnerton.

Annie paused to play with his pup, Blackie. The dog didn't usually warm to anyone except him but, like his master, was captivated by Lady Annia Childe.

Swinnerton stood frowning down at the hound as if the tail-wagging mutt was his rival for her affections. By God, Swinnerton needed to know that Lady Annia Childe was *not* available!

$\mathcal{C}$hapter 6

Bidding his guests farewell was not without regrets. How excited he had been four-and-twenty hours earlier, how eagerly he had looked forward to seeing Annie and to showing her his favorite place. All that promise was unfulfilled, like a beautiful babe grown into pimpled corpulence. Nothing had gone as he'd expected. It filled him with bitterness to think another man had been the one to show her *his* gardens.

Now nothing brought pleasure. As Annie moved to be handed onto the yacht, he stepped up and offered his arm. "Allow me. I shouldn't like to see you take a second plunge, my lady."

"Oh, your grace, I am so sorry." Her hand settled upon his sleeve.

Under normal circumstances, a woman's so modest a touch would not have affected him in the least.

Annie, though, was not just *any* woman. Annie's touch affected him.

"Nothing to apologize for. I am just happy I was able to pull a *live* body from this river."

Once she was on his yacht, Swinnerton

and Crest swooped upon her like birds to breadcrumbs.

His last vision of her was of her waving at him, Swinnerton at one side and Lord Crest at the other where she sat on the long bench.

That same vision would not disappear long after the yacht was out of sight. He went to his library to catch up on his correspondence, but he could not dispel the picture of her being flirted with by not one, but two men.

When he was unable to compose even a passable salutatory sentence, he put his letters aside and pulled a book off the shelf. Since Gibbon's second volume was scheduled to be out any day, he thought to reread the first volume. Even in school, he'd been fond of anything to do with the Romans. That, too, proved futile. All his thoughts were on Annie.

What was to prevent a pretty girl like her from falling in love with either of those men? Could her father not make it clear to her that neither of them was worthy of her hand? Neither of them could ever be compatible with her.

Last night Alex had been confident in her affections. That the daughter of an earl would have ridden in a potato boat indicated a far greater fondness than a mere desire to see Ripley would warrant.

And then, he thought with a hitch in his now-erratic breath, there was The Kiss. It would have been impossible to fake the passion she'd put into that kiss.

So how had he repaid the girl for her affections? He'd fled in the same way an offended schoolgirl might have. It would serve him right if she accepted Swinnerton—or Lord Crest. He'd wager neither of those gentlemen would have rushed away after kissing her.

The notion of her accepting either of them felt like the thump from a cannonball.

He tried to analyze those feelings that had sent him reeling away from her the previous night. He had been bloody afraid his precious bachelorhood was being threatened.

It suddenly became clear to him that bachelorhood could not compare to what he felt for Annie. She possessed every single quality he could ever want in a woman. When she was removed from the Marriage Mart, he could be a shriveled up old man before another could ever offer all that Annie did.

He also examined what was so bloody satisfying about his unwed state. How long had it been since he had looked forward to something with as much eager anticipation as he'd looked forward to showing Ripley to Annie?

All of his possessions were nothing if he could not share them with someone. Someone like Annie.

No, he thought, not someone *like* Annie, he wanted to share all he had with Annie.

He rang for a servant. "We return to

London."

* * *

He found Lord Tolworth at Brook's not long after night fell. "I beg a private word, my lord."

The two men found a quiet chamber and stood before the fire. Alex cleared his throat. "I have reason to believe that your daughter may not be indifferent to my affections." He cleared his throat again. "And there is no man who would value . . . indeed *love* your daughter more than I. Therefore, I seek your permission to . . ." He swallowed. "To marry Lady Annia."

There was a twinkle in Lord Tolworth's eye and a smile on his face. "I always thought you and my Annie would suit. Nothing would give me greater pleasure than to see you two marry."

During the long carriage ride back to London, Alex had given considerable thought to the manner in which he would convey to both Lord Tolworth and to his daughter his intention of wedding her. Now he had a plan.

Alex sighed. "I also seek your assistance in another matter. Can you see that Annie sits in the gallery of the House of Lords tomorrow?"

$\mathcal{C}$hapter 7

Papa had procured for her a seat in the gallery and told her a matter of great import was to be brought up that day. "You can't miss it," he said. "I want you there."

She came with her father to the White Chapel in the Palace of Westminster, and while he took his place at a front bench on the floor, she climbed the narrow staircase to the gallery and took her seat on the front row. How fortuitous. Ordinarily she was not able to obtain so good a seat.

When the Duke of Axminster entered the chamber, something inside of her softened and squiggled. Even were he not a duke, he looked like one who was accustomed to power. Would she ever be able to look at the man and not inwardly sigh from want of him? His dark head stood out from the shorter men surrounding him. Even those men—all peers of the realm—meekened in his presence.

Her breath grew short at the memory of being held in his arms, of kissing him.

Once all the lords were present and seated, Alex stood and began to address the assemblage. "My esteemed colleagues, I stand here before you today to reverse myself. Since I entered this august chamber a decade ago I have consistently opposed our nation's global expansion. Time and time again I have touted isolationism. I have opposed having our military spread across the globe at the expense of leaving our borders not fully protected. I have opposed draining our country of brilliant men who are governing distant lands where the natives' customs differ vastly from our own. I have always maintained that Britain needs nothing from other parts of the world.

"I was wrong."

Voices lifted to fill the chamber.

"Just as a man—possibly even a duke," he continued, pausing to look up into the gallery. Their eyes met. "Cannot exist in a vacuum, our country cannot continue to prosper if we are isolated. Just as a man can never know true happiness without a woman with whom he can share his life, our country is stronger for its connections with diverse civilizations." He finally removed his gaze from hers.

Her heartbeat accelerated. What did he mean *possibly a duke*? Or *man can never know true happiness without a woman with whom he can share his life*? Could he be referring to himself?

And why had he not been able to remove his gaze from hers?

He continued, "For it is those connections that give us our precious tea, sugar, and fine silks. It is those connections which expand our knowledge of the human race. It is those connections which give this, the greatest nation in the world, the opportunity to spread our knowledge and our vast resources to make the world a better place.

"It is our obligation to embrace expansion—expansion without bloodshed. Standing alone—whether it be a country or a man—weakens us."

Now his gaze returned to her. "Therefore, I stand before you today a changed man, a man committed to expanding—even to expanding my family—if it is not too late. Only you can say if I have the right."

The room went silent, and the other Lords followed his gaze up to the gallery and eyed her. Why wasn't he finishing his speech? Was he waiting for some kind of response from her? Dear Lord in heaven! Was he asking her to marry him?

She did not know what to do. She did not want to read something into his words that wasn't there. How embarrassing it would be to make a fool of herself.

But was it not better to risk embarrassment on the hope of becoming betrothed to the man of her dreams?

She stood, holding on to the railing with trembling hands, her gaze riveted to his. And she nodded.

He smiled, then looking away, he continued. "The Bible says, *Be fruitful and increase in numbers*. Let us, esteemed colleagues, do as the Bible instructs us. Let us embrace our fellow man—no matter where that man might originate. Let us spread our British intellect to lands near and far. Let us reap the benefits of trade. For expansion will keep us the mightiest nation on earth."

Once again, his gaze lifted to hers. "And it will make me the happiest man on earth."

* * *

Long after the floor of the chamber cleared, long after everyone left the gallery, she sat there, dazed.

Then he came to her. "They'll be snuffing all the candles soon."

She nodded. "I suppose Papa's waiting for me."

"No, your father left. He has given me permission to bring you home in my carriage." Alex came and took both her hands in his. "He has also given me permission to ask for your hand in marriage. Was your nod what I think it was?"

She was trembling even more now as she nodded.

He drew her into his arms and kissed her. If possible, this kiss was even more passionate than the last.

"I was afraid you did not find me skilled in

kissing," she whispered when they finished.

"My dearest love, that is not why I so abruptly left. I left because your kisses were so skillful as to inflame me."

She wrapped her arms around him and lay her face against his powerful chest. Nothing had ever felt so wonderful.

"My God, Annie, I love you." He kissed her again.

"And I love you," she said when they finished.

"Your father believes we were made for each other."

"My father and I have always thought alike."

$\mathcal{E}$pilogue

On the eve of their wedding, Lady Tolworth had requested a private meeting with Annie and Alex. The betrothed couple sat on a settee in the family parlor, holding hands when her ladyship strolled into the chamber.

"It's time I pass on the Roman ring," Lady Tolworth said. "It's my hope you will be the next in a very long line of wearers, my dearest."

Annie's chest tightened. She knew she could not be the recipient of the ring unless both of them were truly in love. No woman in the kingdom could be more completely in love than she, and she believed Alex loved her in the same way.

The ring will tell. What would she do if it darkened? For that would mean Alex was not truly in love with her. Her grip on his hand strengthened as her mother came closer.

Lady Tolworth removed the ring. "Here, dearest, let's see if you and his grace love each other as your father and I have loved these many years." She drew in a breath. "But if it should darken, do not let that come between you."

If it darkened, the ring would go to Fanny later—if Fanny found a true love.

"It won't darken," Annie said with confidence. She took the ring.

Before she could put it on, Alex said, "Allow me, my love." He took the ring and slipped it upon the third finger of her right hand.

Three sets of eyes watched in silence for a few moments. It stayed ruby red.

Lady Tolworth broke the silence. "I'm confident it won't change." Her gaze swung from Annie to Alex. "Anyone who sees you knows how truly you love one another." She hugged Annie. "I know you'll be very happy."

Alex's arm came around his intended. "You are loved."

"As are you, my dearest soon-to-be husband." She loved the way that sounded.

It was then that Annie saw the door was open a crack. Fanny had been watching. "You might as well come in," she told her sister.

Fanny came strolling into the chamber. "It's really not fair that *you* get the Roman ring when I'm the oldest."

"You are not!"

"Come now, girls," Lady Tolworth said. "Let your last night together be free from arguing."

Alex rose. "Since it's your last night with your sister, I will leave."

She walked him to the door and he drew her into his arms. "All the rest of the nights of our lives, you will spend with me," he murmured.

THE END

Cheryl Bolen's Regency romance series:

Brazen Brides Series
Counterfeit Countess (Book 1)
His Golden Ring (Book 2)
Oh What A (Wedding) Night (Book 3)
Marriage of Inconvenience (Book 4)

House of Haverstock Series
Lady by Chance (Book 1)
Duchess by Mistake (Book2)
Countess by Coincidence (Book 3)

The Brides of Bath Series:
The Bride Wore Blue (Book 1)
With His Ring (Book 2)
The Bride's Secret (Book 3)
To Take This Lord (Book 4)
Love in the Library (Book 5)
A Christmas in Bath (Book 6)

The Regent Mysteries Series:
With His Lady's Assistance (Book 1)
A Most Discreet Inquiry (Book 2)
The Theft Before Christmas (Book 3)
An Egyptian Affair (Book 4)

Author's Biography

A former journalist and English teacher, Cheryl Bolen sold her first book to Harlequin Historical in 1997. That book, *A Duke Deceived*, was a finalist for the Holt Medallion for Best First Book, and it netted her the title Notable New Author. Since then she has published more than 20 books with Kensington/Zebra, Love Inspired Historical and was Montlake launch author for Kindle Serials. As an independent author, she has broken into the top 5 on the *New York Times* and top 20 on the *USA Today* bestseller lists.

Her 2005 book *One Golden Ring* won the Holt Medallion for Best Historical, and her 2011 gothic historical *My Lord Wicked* was awarded Best Historical in the International Digital Awards, the same year one of her Christmas novellas was chosen as Best Historical Novella by Hearts Through History. Her books have been finalists for other awards, including the Daphne du Maurier, and have been translated into eight languages.

She invites readers to www.CherylBolen.com, or her blog, www.cherylsregencyramblings.wordpress.co or Facebook at https://www.facebook.com/pages/Cheryl-Bolen-Books/146842652076424.